A SHOT FROM THE SHADOWS

Moonlight was the only illumination. There was a thump of hoofs and the clicking of horns as the cattle inside the pen tried to jump away from each other in the corral. The figure was indistinct in the darkness. Black on charcoal: drooping hat brim, the shotgun seen in uncertain silhouette canted across the chest and belly.

But Longarm knew. And so did the man with the gun. The shotgun came up, the range closer than Longarm would have believed possible for anyone to get without being seen before now. Longarm reached for his Colt.

The gun barked—and a sheet of fire lit up the rough timber of the loading chute, and sent the beeves into a sudden panic . . .

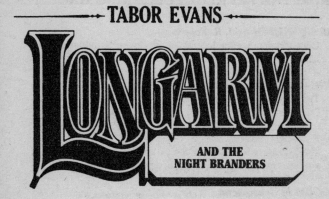

TABOR EVANS

LONGARM

AND THE
NIGHT BRANDERS

JOVE BOOKS, NEW YORK

LONGARM AND THE NIGHT BRANDERS

A Jove Book / published by arrangement with
the author

PRINTING HISTORY
Jove edition / January 1993

All rights reserved.
Copyright © 1993 by Jove Publications, Inc.
This book may not be reproduced in whole
or in part, by mimeograph or any other means,
without permission. For information address:
The Berkley Publishing Group, 200 Madison Avenue,
New York, New York 10016.

ISBN: 0-515-11018-3

Jove Books are published by The Berkley Publishing Group,
200 Madison Avenue, New York, New York 10016.
The name "JOVE" and the "J" logo
are trademarks belonging to Jove Publications, Inc.

PRINTED IN THE UNITED STATES OF AMERICA

10 9 8 7 6 5 4 3 2 1

Chapter 1

Deputy U.S. Marshal Custis Long dipped two fingers into a vest pocket and extracted his reliable and ever accurate Ingersoll timepiece. The watch quite accurately and reliably confirmed what his stomach already told him: It was well past noon, already much of the way through the normal dinner hour, and still he was being kept waiting in the outer office of the United States Marshal, Justice Department, Denver District, William "Billy" Vail.

"Y' don't suppose . . . ," he started, but the marshal's bespectacled and sometimes prissy clerk Henry cut him off with a dark look and the information—not new—that "He knows you're here."

"Yeah, sure." Longarm stood, feeling as much restless as he was hungry, and paced the small room for a few minutes. He lighted a slim, dark-leafed cheroot that he puffed on. The activity did little to alleviate his restlessness, and the smoke did nothing to assuage his hunger. Custis Long simply did not care for the inactivity of sitting about in an office and waiting for something to happen.

After a few minutes he stopped before Henry's desk. "Look, I could grab a quick bite an' be back here in just—"

"No." The clerk didn't even look up from what he was doing. Which, Longarm could see now, had to do with the expense vouchers submitted by the deputies who worked out of this office. The particular form Henry happened to be working on at the moment looked somewhat familiar.

Longarm turned away. But not in time.

"A dollar twenty-five cents it says here? For a seamstress?"

"That was the Robideaux warrant. It's in my report. When I put the cuffs on the guy, his girlfriend went crazy. She ripped the pocket off my coat. Here. If you turn it inside out an' look real close you can see what a nice job that lady did fixing it. See?" He sidled closer to Henry's desk and turned to one side, offering the coat pocket as evidence. "See?"

Henry grunted disapprovingly.

"Dang it, I couldn't very well walk around with my pocket torn half off an' hanging down, could I? An' it did happen in the line o' duty."

"Lots of things seem to happen to you in the line of duty," Henry commented.

"That ain't my fault, is it?"

"I'll answer that if you really want me to. But you might not agree with my opinion on the subject."

"In that case, never mind."

Longarm went back to his pacing, and Henry continued on with his paperwork.

Although there were two men in the office, a visitor might only have noticed one. Henry was quiet and plain, the sort who easily becomes lost in a crowd. Custis Long was neither plain nor unobtrusive.

Billy Vail's top deputy stood four inches over six feet tall, and had a broad-shouldered, narrow-hipped, horseman's lean build. He had brown hair and dark, piercing brown eyes, a wide sweep of handlebar mustache, and the tanned, leathery complexion that comes from years spent exposed to sun, wind, rain, and cold.

He wore a brown tweed coat—recently repaired—and tall, stovepipe cavalry boots with low heels meant for walking comfort. He had on khaki trousers and a calfskin vest with a slender gold chain linking the two pockets. At one end of the chain was his trusty Ingersoll watch, at the other an equally trusty but seldom displayed .44-caliber derringer with two barrels and an unpleasant disposition.

A .44-40 double-action Colt revolver rode in a cross-draw rig just to the left of his belt buckle, the worn butt canted to the side for a swift and fluid right-hand draw.

At the moment he wasn't feeling cranky and ornery enough to draw down on anybody with the big Colt. But he almost wished that Henry would think he was, just so maybe that would prompt Henry to stir the boss along.

Longarm stopped pacing, disposed of his cigar butt in a small container of sand put out for that purpose, and once more checked his watch. Very few minutes had gone by since the last time he looked. "Dammit, Henry, I—"

The door to Billy's private office opened, and one of the governor's more obnoxious aides paraded through with his nose aimed toward the ceiling.

"Y' know," Longarm said before the hall door closed behind the political ass-wiper, "ol' Barry there always walks like he's got a chunk o' cob hung up where he can't get a good grip t' pull it out. Ever notice that?"

Henry sent a mortified glance toward the partially open door. And then, as finally the door sealed closed and he could be sure that Barry would not hear, he began to laugh. "If that was your way of making yourself popular with the movers and shakers in this state, Longarm, then I think you could benefit from some lessons in tact."

"No, what I could benefit from is some less, not some lessons. Less shit-for-brains suck-ups like that one, for instance. Less state idjits trying to mix into our federal affairs, for another. Whyn't you tell me what was going on in there?"

"Because, darn you, you would have insisted on barging in and insulting the governor's representative."

"The governor's representative farts in his bathwater an' bites the bubbles. I have that on good authority."

"He probably does," Henry agreed, "but Marshal Vail has enough to worry about right now without you adding to his problems."

"Political shit again?" Longarm asked. If there was anything in this world that he despised, it was when politics got in the way of the job. Law enforcement was hard enough without a bunch of amateurs trying to reshape right and wrong for their own purposes.

"Again? Still," Henry said.

Longarm shook his head. "Sometimes I don't know how he puts up with it."

"Which is probably why he is the marshal and you are the deputy."

"What about the marshal?" Billy Vail asked from the doorway of his office. Billy was red-faced and balding. The recent years spent indoors behind a desk had given him a paunch, and he no longer looked half as salty as he really was. Vail was no mere political appointee to his position, though. He was a former Ranger, a former deputy with extensive field experience, and a dedicated, solidly professional peace officer who kept his position by being very, very good at it. Billy Vail had the respect as well as the loyalty of the deputies who rode for him. "What were you two yammering about out here?"

"Nothing, sir," Henry said.

"Nothing, Boss," Longarm concurred. "You, uh, wanted t' see me?"

4

"I did, but that . . ." Billy paused and swallowed. "That gentleman there insisted on telling me the same thing five times over."

"There's a rule 'bout that, you know," Longarm said. "If you're told something five times, then you're honor-bound t' believe it."

Billy made a face and rolled his eyes. "I still want to talk to you, Longarm, but personally I'm hungry. Have you had dinner yet?"

"Nope."

"Then grab your hat and come with me. You too, Henry. My treat."

"Somehow, Boss, I got the idea this ain't entirely an accidental occasion," Longarm observed.

"Whatever gives you that impression?" Billy asked, his eyes wide and innocent.

"Just a hunch," Longarm said. "An' knowing that not a hell of a lot happens 'round here except for the way you plan it." He lifted his snuff-brown Stetson down from the hat rack, though, and tugged it into place. "Ready when you boys are, I reckon."

Chapter 2

Once they were out of the Federal Building and started east on
Colfax toward Denver's Capitol Hill area, Billy Vail unbent
with his two favorite employees—and friends—enough to
grouse and grumble a little.

"They never want much, you know. Just an inch here. And
another there. And then a few more somewhere else. It's like
being caught in a piece of string. It doesn't seem like much
until all of a sudden you wake up and realize you're wrapped
so tight in the stuff that you can't move anymore."

"You're talking about the governor's man?" Henry asked.
"Or the governor himself?" Longarm only half heard the
conversation. He was concentrating on the rather intriguing
side-to-side hip sway of a yellow-haired lady walking several
dozen paces in front of them.

"There is never anything you could run back to the big man,"
Billy said. "You know that. It's always hints, innuendoes, and
intimations with these people. But of course I know what it's
all about."

"What's that?" Henry asked. Longarm was disappointed. The
lady—or not, one couldn't always tell by looking—turned off
into a store front, leaving the view ahead to consist of nothing

6

more interesting than mud-spattered carriages and boys selling newspapers.

"I'm being asked to use my manpower on a fool's mission. They seem to think it's all right for *us* to appear foolish but not *them.*"

"What mission is that?" Again it was Henry who asked.

"The suggestion—not a request, mind, but only a suggestion—is that I use my staff to conduct an undercover investigation of the labor movement in the coal mines down south."

"But that is strictly a state concern," Henry protested. "We have no federal jurisdiction to enter into labor-management disputes even if we wanted to. Nor would we have enough manpower to take on something like that."

"As it happens," Billy agreed, "I lack both the inclination and the wherewithal. But the suggestion was made. They knew I would reject it, of course. So another was made in parting, probably under the assumption that having refused to help once I couldn't very well turn around and refuse them again. This time it has to do with relinquishing a prosecution so the state can pursue the case instead."

"Which you also refused?"

Billy frowned. "Which I haven't refused, actually. Haven't decided either way. I mean, it's a very minor case they want us to pass up. And I think I understand how the governor expects to gain."

"Favorable press?" Henry guessed.

"Nothing so straightforward," Billy said. Longarm's interest perked up. A young couple stepped out onto the sidewalk ahead of them. The girl, though, turned out to have a complexion like a boiled pudding. And a figure like one too. His attention returned to the chatter between Billy and Henry.

"The governor wants to pass a bill to fund public education this next legislative session. Which would be good, of course, although the particular methods he wants will line the pockets of his very good friends as much as it will provide for school funding. Really, I suppose this plan isn't any worse than most. But as you may know, it is being opposed on the senate floor by George Walker from Douglas County. This jurisdictional thing is a gift to Walker. For some reason the senator's fiancée wants this matter in question to be handled as a state case. I believe a relative of hers might be in line for an appointment as a special prosecutor or something like that. Anyway, that's what they want. They want us to relinquish our interest in this case . . . it's a simple enough thing, theft of government property, theft of a horse owned by a government survey party if it matters . . . so the state can prosecute the accused as a horse thief."

"It sounds like you're inclined to give them what they want," Henry observed.

"In a way I suppose I am. It really does seem a small enough favor from where we stand. On the other hand, it would matter a very great deal to the accused. A conviction for theft of U.S. government property might result in one to three years' incarceration. Conviction of horse theft under Colorado law could conceivably be punished by hanging. That hasn't happened in a state court in some time. But the law is still on the books, and you never know where a judge and jury may go. I suppose my reluctance in the matter has to do more with exposing some poor SOB to a capital prosecution than it does with questioning the political motives of our, um, colleagues in the capitol building."

"It isn't something you have to decide right away, is it?" Henry asked.

"No. The vote on that educational funding bill won't come up for several months. On the other hand, the governor wants to know that Walker will be in his corner when the time comes. I suppose I should give them an answer reasonably soon, as a simple courtesy if nothing else. Ah. Here we are."

Longarm didn't recognize the building Billy claimed was their destination. But then he hadn't been paying all that much attention to where they were going while they walked. Once he looked around to get his bearings he realized they had turned onto a shaded, little-traveled side street and that the place where they were now entering—it looked more like a residence than a restaurant—was a private club. He had heard about this particular club but hadn't known his boss was a member. Membership was definitely for the nabobs and the political heavyweights. Billy Vail was commencing to run in fast company if he was making himself a part of this crowd. It was just that sort of thing that made Longarm glad he was only a deputy and not the bossman.

Once inside they were greeted by a tall, swarthy man, probably one of Denver's many Italian immigrants, who had a huge mustache and an even larger smile. The man bowed low and said, "Marshal Vail, so nice to see you today, sir. Your table is ready."

The table was indeed ready, and had been before they ever arrived. And set for three, Longarm noticed.

"Correct me if I'm wrong, Boss, but you're wanting something from Henry an' me. An' we ain't gonna like it much. If it's got something t' do with that political bullshit . . ."

"No, Longarm, nothing at all to do with that, I assure you," Vail said quickly. "Now why don't we not worry about business until later, hmm? We're in no hurry here."

That was enough to make even Henry lift an eyebrow. Billy Vail being so casual about office hours and the pressures of duty? Why, anyone would have to think twice about that.

Still, Billy insisted that they enjoy a nice lunch with him. And a very nice lunch it was too. The foods were rich and heavy enough to put a man into a stupor. But then perhaps that was the whole idea. Longarm was skeptical. But he wasn't going to pass up a good meal because of it. He waded into the groceries till the

9

juice dripped off his elbows—figuratively speaking, anyway—then leaned back with his legs extended and ankles crossed to enjoy a fine cheroot and an after-dinner tot of rye whiskey. If this was a form of bribery, then he figured he could sure as hell be bought.

Billy, Longarm thought, was stalling. Whatever was on the boss's mind, he was having trouble coming out with it now. Lunch was over, the dishes all cleared away, and the last drinks poured. And still Billy seemed to be having trouble getting to the point of all this.

Finally the marshal ran a finger under his collar, coughed once into his fist, and reached inside his coat to extract a folded paper and hand it to Henry.

"I'd like you to file this," he said. "It is, um, evidence."

Papers that needed filing weren't generally delivered in gentlemen's private clubs. But Henry took the document and started to tuck it out of sight inside his own coat. "You can look at it first," Billy said. "The date in particular is important."

Henry shrugged and looked at the paper.

"Longarm should see the date too," Billy said. Henry handed the sheet across the table to Longarm.

The paper, Longarm saw, was a conveyance of title, signed by a party named E. M. Parks, dated six weeks earlier, giving ownership of four beeves to the United States government, Department of the Interior, Bureau of Indian Affairs, and asking that said beeves be donated for use by needy children at an Indian agency of the government's choosing.

"Okay, Boss, we both seen it," Longarm said, handing the document back to Henry, who folded it and tucked it away out of sight. "Now whyn't you tell us what it means?"

Billy really did not look comfortable now. He looked—it took Longarm a minute or so to get a handle on it—he looked embarrassed.

He was always pink in the face. Now he was heated up to a bright glowing red like a stove stuffed overfull with fat pitch pine.

"You can, um, you can both see from that grant of title that, um, the beeves in question were and, uh, have been the property of the United States since the, um, date recorded there."

"Billy," Longarm said, "me an' Henry ain't stupid. What you're doing here is going way the hell out on some wee tiny limb so you can find an excuse t' take jurisdiction over something."

"Well . . . yes."

"Dammit, Billy, we'll go along with whatever you want. You know that. You don't have t' go through all this crap t' convince us o' anything. Just tell us what you want done an' we'll do our best t' see to it."

"This particular matter is uncomfortably . . . personal," Vail confessed.

"Shit, we guessed that much already."

"Longarm is right," Henry put in. "You don't have to make excuses to either of us."

"To myself then," Billy said. "I shouldn't ask you to involve yourselves. But I can't . . . refuse to do something to help. And it simply would not be possible for me to take charge of this myself. I would if I could. But I . . . I just can't. It wouldn't be fair. It wouldn't be at all right."

"We don't neither of us have any idea what the hell you're talking about, Billy," Longarm said.

"No, of course you don't." Vail sighed. He looked around, caught a waiter's eye, and motioned toward his wine glass. Not until his wine and Longarm's rye and Henry's chilled apple cider were refilled did he try to explain.

"You both know my wife," he said. "She is . . . very dear to me. You know that. I would literally prefer to die before I would dishonor her. But she was not the first nor the only

11

love in my life. Once . . . it seems a long time ago now . . . once there was someone else. I would have proposed to her then, but we quarreled about something. Never mind what. The fact is, we had a quarrel. A foolish one, as all lovers' quarrels are, I suppose. And then it was too late. She married someone else, and we went our separate ways. I saw her once, after the war. By then, of course, I too had married. That time we parted as friends. More or less." Billy's hand trembled a little, Longarm thought, when he reached for his wine glass.

"I didn't see her again for years. Then late last year while on an excursion train to Palmer Lake, I happened to see her again at the railroad depot. The meeting was entirely innocent. I learned that she was a widow. She already knew that I was in Denver, but of course she also knew that I was . . . that I *am* . . . quite happily married. She hadn't intended to contact me. Nor did she seek any personal communication again. Then . . . two months ago, I believe it was, she came to me. In desperation. She felt she had no choice. She is, as I said, a widow. Her circumstances are what you might call precarious. Roy left her with a small holding of land and dairy cattle. She is not poor, certainly, but there is little surplus. She can continue to provide for herself if she is allowed to do so. But since Roy died she has suffered occasional losses of livestock. Dairy-bred steers, for the most part. They have been stolen from her. Her complaints to the local authorities have produced no result. They find her losses too minor to much bother with. And of course they are minor in one sense. But devastating to her if allowed to continue unchecked." Billy finished off that glass of wine and signaled for another.

"I can understand the sheriff's office not wanting to waste his manpower on a five-dollar dairy steer. But to Eudora that five-dollar steer represents the difference between comfort and poverty for the month. And a pattern of continuing losses could drive her beyond the brink and ruin her completely. I . . . could

12

not in good conscience allow that risk to go unchecked. But I cannot take action myself without dishonoring, or seeming to, the woman I most care for. I find myself impaled on the horns of a dilemma, caught between my obligations to my wife and to Eudora too."

Eudora, Longarm thought. E for Eudora, E as in E. M. Parks.

"And since cattle theft ain't a federal crime," Longarm jumped in, "you suggested she deed over a couple culls an' hope one of 'em was stolen, because once a cow owned by the Department o' the Interior got carried off, then there was federal jurisdiction an' you could do something to help. Except now it's gone an' actually happened an' you're thinking that you're using your office for personal reasons, an' now you've got all shy 'bout your own damn-fool idea. Does that about cover the ground, Billy?"

Vail blushed and bobbed his head. "Something like that, yes."

"Henry, what wants an' warrants do we have down toward where Miz Parks lives? We got any?"

"I believe there are several writs that could be served in that neighborhood, Longarm."

"An' if I went down there t' serve them papers an' happened t' stumble over something related t' this problem Miz Parks is having?"

"Then it would certainly be within the normal scope of your duties to pursue the matter, wouldn't it?" Henry answered.

Longarm looked at Billy and grinned. "See there? It ain't so complicated after all."

Vail looked from one of them to the other and back again. "There isn't much greater a blessing in any man's life than to have good friends," he said. "Thank you. Thank you both."

"Aw, it's no trouble at all, Boss. No trouble a'tall."

Which was a lie of the very first water, but he had no way to know that at the time.

Chapter 3

Longarm checked his coat pockets, and was reassured to feel the crinkling bulk of folded papers that represented half a dozen warrants there. He reset the cheroot in a corner of his jaw, tugged once at the collar of his shirt and once at the brim of his hat, and picked up his carpetbag with one hand and his McClellan saddle with the other; he was thus prepared to disembark from the train at the Lark Ranch spur and get to work.

"You sure you want to get off here, Marshal?" the conductor asked him for probably the eighth time.

"I'm sure, Ned. Although I thank you for your concern. Really, though, it will be all right." The tall deputy grinned. "After all, it isn't like you're abandoning me a hundred miles from civilization. If I really have to I can just follow the tracks south across the divide to Monument, or else go back north to Castle Rock. They aren't either one of 'em more than, what? A dozen miles or so?"

"I just don't feel right about putting a passenger off here, Marshal." The conductor was a friendly fellow if sometimes a touch on the nervous side. Longarm probably had ridden on his coaches a dozen times, often enough for a nodding sort of acquaintance, although he doubted he had ever heard Ned's last name. Or if he had he had since forgotten it. Ned, for his part, seemed to think of the federal deputy as something of a celebrity and was always eager to be of help whenever he could.

"This siding spur makes it okay to stop here, right?" Longarm said.

"Oh, there's no reason it can't be done. I just don't like doing it, there not being a station here or anything. Look, I tell you what. There's a covered box near the siding switch. We keep oil in there for the signal lamps, grease, odds and ends like that. We also keep some booms in there."

"Booms?"

"You know. Signal booms."

"Bombs," Longarm said.

"Yeah. That's what I just told you. Booms."

"Right," Longarm agreed. "Booms."

"Yeah. The thing is, if you want the train to stop here an' pick you up or something, you take a couple of those booms and lay them on the tracks, one a half mile out and the other a mile away. That's all you got to do is lay them on the track. When the lead wheel runs over one it explodes it. Not so much of a charge as to hurt anything, of course, but it makes a helluva noise. The engineer hears those booms go off before the siding an' he knows he's to stop."

"Of course I have to already know the train schedule, don't I?" Longarm asked. "Otherwise how would I know if I should lay the booms out to the north to catch a southbound, or set them out the other way to signal a northbound train?"

The conductor frowned and scratched behind his right ear. "I never thought of that." Then he brightened. "You could put booms out in both directions if it's some kinda emergency and you need to stop the next train through. You could do that."

"You know, Ned, you're absolutely right. I should've thought o' that myself. Thanks."

15

The conductor grinned and bobbed his head, obviously feeling better now that he'd given this rather special passenger a method by which a return to civilization might be made.

Longarm smiled to himself and didn't bother to comment further. After all, the man meant entirely well. It was just that apparently Ned, whose railroad cars traveled through miles upon miles of very empty country each and every day, was one of those for whom it was unthinkable that a person might survive—for hours at a time, never mind days—without the continuous presence of walls and roofs and other folks within hailing distance.

Probably Ned would have been terrified at the thought of anyone striking out afoot into the mountains that loomed so close to the west, or even nonchalantly and without fear choosing to hike across the rolling grassland prairie that began at the base of those mountains and spread eastward, unbroken and untrammeled and largely uninhabited, from here all the way to Kansas City.

Longarm, fortunately, was not victim to those fears. Empty country to him meant freedom, not shadowy dangers. Why, there was nothing a man need fear in this broad and beautiful country. Not in the way of wild beasts, anyway. All the seemingly scary animals, the great cats and bears and very few remaining wolves, were much too shy and timid themselves to engage in any fight not forced upon them. And in truth even the human population in open country tended to be much more welcoming than sinister. More so, perhaps, than could be said about folks in the cities. The only remaining thing anyone could possibly worry about when alone would be weather or accident. And Longarm certainly wasn't going to worry about such unlikely concerns when he was less than half a day's walk from the nearest towns.

What he was going to do was remember to be appreciative of the conductor's concern and simply let it go at that.

The Denver & Rio Grande mixed train of passenger and freight coaches clanked and shuddered to a jerky halt within a hundred yards of the skeletal iron switch bar and tall, gallows-like railroad signal pole that marked the Lark Ranch siding.

Ned unlatched the coach door and lowered the steel boarding steps. "Are you *sure*, Marshal, you don't want me to leave train orders for someone to pick you up? Why, I—"

"I'm fine, Ned. I promise you. I'll just walk over to John Lark's place an' see can I borrow the use of a horse. And if there's no one home there, why, there's plenty of folks with smaller spreads close around here. I won't have any trouble. Really." Longarm stepped down onto the bed of lumpy ballast gravel that lined the tracks, and Ned got down too.

"All right," the conductor reluctantly allowed. "But don't forget about those—"

"Booms," Longarm finished for him. "I won't forget about the booms, Ned, and if I need to stop a train I'll use them. Thanks. And I mean that. Thanks a lot." Longarm set down his saddle to free his hand to shake, then winked at the conductor and jauntily retrieved the lightweight McClellan—hard on a rider but easy on a horse's back—with the scabbard and Winchester buckled in place.

Ned hopped back onto the coach steps and signaled forward to the engineer. The steam engine hissed and snorted as power was fed to the huge driving wheels, and slowly the train began to move, one car at a time clattering into motion as slack was noisily taken up in the couplings and the immense power of the locomotive was applied. The conductor pulled the folding steps inside the car, but leaned out once more before he closed the coach door.

"Don't forget, Marshal," he called out as the train began to gather speed. "If you need help . . ."

"Thank you, Ned. Bye." Longarm had no hand free to wave with. He waited a moment until the well-intentioned Ned was

17

far enough away that he was unlikely to see, then shook his head in amusement. It must be terrible, he thought, to be so frightened of being alone and without the protection of walls.

Longarm swung his saddle and rifle to his shoulder and, cheroot riding at a cocky angle, began to amble quite contentedly in the direction of the Lark Ranch.

Chapter 4

"Oh golly, Custis, is that really *you*!" The porch door of the Lark home banged open, and a blond-headed, pigtailed catamount came tearing out with a rush and a roar. Blond-headed, anyway. Pigtailed, certainly. And catamount? Well, she seemed like one at the time.

Longarm braced himself for the assault and dropped his bag so he would have an arm free.

The girl launched herself into the air a good five feet before she reached him, and was chest high when she hit. She clamped her arms tight around Longarm's neck, and it was pure self-defense for him to take a wrap around her waist with his newly freed left arm.

"So, Cathy Sue. Are you still mad at me?"

She squealed and let go of her hold on his neck so she could lean back and begin pummeling his chest with both fists.

Longarm took care of that by dropping her.

She slid down his body to ground level, let out a shriek, and hit him another couple of licks in the belly. That accomplished, she jumped onto him again and planted a kiss full on his mouth.

"Now dang it, Cathy Sue, you know—"

"Hush." She kissed him again, with more exuberance than expertise, and then said, "I *was* mad, Custis, but I've decided to forgive you."

"Thanks, I'm sure."

"Now be quiet and kiss me."

He gave her a peck on the cheek.

"Not like that. Like this." She covered his mouth with her own, and this time he was startled to feel the girl's tongue probe beyond his teeth and on in the general direction of his tonsils.

"Cathy Sue," he warned.

"Don't start that again, Custis. Just don't you dare. Maybe you had good reason last time, but you don't anymore. Think about that."

"If you'll climb down off'n me, girl, could be I will."

"Will what?"

"Think about what you just said."

"Okay, that's fair." But she didn't go right away. First she kissed him again. And this time, dammit, he couldn't much help responding to the insistent heat of her lips and tongue.

He did, in fact, commence to get a hard-on.

Which Cathy Sue didn't help when she slid down over the bulging thing on her way back to ground level.

"Oh, my. Did I do that?"

So much for the hope that she might not've noticed.

"Reckon you did."

She beamed as if that was just about the nicest compliment she'd received since Christmas past. "Really?"

"Quit now, Cathy Sue. That isn't ladylike."

"A lady isn't what I'm wanting to be like, Custis Long. Not right now it isn't."

"Well, try an' do it anyway. For your daddy's sake."

"Daddy wouldn't know a lady if he fell into one's bed."

20

"If your daddy fell into one's bed, then that'n wouldn't be much of a lady, would she?"

"Anyway, it isn't no lady I'm wanting to be when I'm with you, Custis. An' what Daddy doesn't know, Daddy won't be hurt by."

"Then try an' be ladylike for my sake."

"Ha. That's even funnier."

"Dang it, girl, you know me 'most too well, don't you." He reached out, and would have ruffled her hair the way he always used to do. Then abruptly he stopped, his hand frozen in midair, as it occurred to him that Cathy Sue was no long a child and no longer fit for such passing casual gestures as the pat on a backside or the ruffling of her blond locks. "That's . . . kinda what you were tryin' to tell me, ain't it, girl?"

"That I'm growing up? Yes, Custis, it is. I'm not a little girl anymore. I haven't been for a long time. Not even two years ago when you wouldn't take me to bed an' I got so mad at you about it. Remember, Custis?"

"Oh, I remember, all right. It ain't something I could so easy forget."

"I got mad at you then, Custis, but I saw later you were only trying to protect me. I understand that. But Custis, that was two years ago. And that was at my sixteenth birthday party. I'm eighteen now, Custis. I'm old enough to be taken to wife. Or to bed. And I'll tell you right straight out. I might not be any man's wife, but I'm not a virgin either. I've laid up in the hayloft with Billy Sime and with Carlton Bennett and once with . . . well, never mind. The point is, I'm not a virgin anymore, Custis. I'm a woman. And most every night for as long as I can remember I've thought about what it would be t' be your woman, t' be in your bed with your body pressed hard and hot over mine an' your mouth on my nipples an' your pecker sliding around deep inside my belly where all the squishy-squirmy funny feelings are. You know it's true what

21

I'm telling you, Custis, because I told it all to you two years ago, and it hasn't changed the least little bit since then. It's still you I think about whenever I get wet and hot between my legs, and it's still you that I see when I close my eyes whenever I'm with one of those boys I told you about. It's you, Custis, and it always has been. I'm old enough now, and I want you to take me, Custis. Please?"

It was quite a speech for such a little girl, and it touched him.

And hell, he supposed she was old enough. It was just that Cathy Sue was such a tiny wee little bit of a thing that she looked like a young'un even if she wasn't one any longer.

She was eighteen years old now. That was true once he thought about it, for the last time he'd been here was just over two years ago, and the occasion for the party then had been Cathy Sue's sixteenth birthday, just like she said.

But dag nab it, the girl couldn't stand more than four-foot-seven, four-foot-eight. If she had shoes on. He doubted she weighed more than a good sack of corn meal. Eighty-five pounds if he was going to guess.

She had a little-girl face and a little-girl figure—so far as he could see at this point anyhow—and a high-pitched little-girl voice.

But in truth, dammit, there was no reason at all why he should keep on thinking that the person behind that little-girl face and inside that little-girl body was still the little girl he remembered from years and years back.

He sighed and his hand resumed its motion. But now, instead of ruffling her hair, he cupped Cathy Sue's chin in his palm and tipped her face up. He leaned down and gently, slowly but quite, quite thoroughly, kissed her.

After a moment he felt her knees sag, and she had to grab his wrist to keep her balance.

"Whew!" she whispered when he pulled away. "See, Custis? That's what I been dreaming about all this time."

He smiled. "You sure know how t' make a fella feel good, ma'am. Come the cloudy days when everything in the whole wide world looks gloomy an' vile, I think I'll know now where t' come for the cure."

"I'd do that too, Custis, if I could. I'd do anything for you."

"I b'lieve you would at that, Cathy Sue."

"I wasn't funning you."

"No, I suppose you weren't." He smiled and kissed her again, not quite so thoroughly this time. Then he said, "Judging from the way you been acting out here in the middle of your daddy's yard, I reckon I can take it that he ain't home at the moment?"

"He rode into town to put an order in at the store. He'll not be back till tomorrow morning if I know him, Custis. He'll stop for a drink an' that'll lead to a game of poker or maybe some faro, and then he'll want another drink an' pretty soon one of them painted ladies—which aren't really ladies any more than I am—will catch his eye, and right there on the spot all his good intentions will get wiped away. So in answer to your question, no, Daddy isn't here an' won't be till tomorrow about three, four hours past daybreak."

"Where are the hands then?"

"We only got one hand at the moment. That's Benny. You remember him?"

Longarm nodded. Cathy Sue said, "Benny hasn't changed much. He tries, but he hasn't changed much. Soon as he knew Daddy'd headed for Castle Rock, Benny saddled a fresh horse and went larruping off at a high lope for Monument. I don't expect to see him back till about an hour before Daddy gets here."

"Anybody else here at all, or did they leave you for the varmints to carry off?"

She grinned. "You're the only varmint on the place right now. Netty is here, though. She's got a chicken simmering on the stove, and by the time you and me sit down to eat it there'll be dumplings in the pot and some fresh greens on the side. That's where she is right now, down in the creek bottom looking for greens to pick."

"Chicken an' dumplings, huh?"

"And me for dessert after."

"You got t' give me a little time t' catch up with the notion that you've growed up, Cathy Sue."

She smiled and came onto her tiptoes with her face lifted. Not subtle but effective. He bent down and kissed her. "You have plenty of time, Custis. All the way till after supper when Netty cleans up an' goes back to her shanty."

"You're all heart, Cathy Sue."

"Yes, Custis. An' all of it for you too." She linked her arm in his, and they walked side by side to the house.

Chapter 5

Longarm heard the slam of the back door and the sound of Netty's clodhoppers cross the porch and down the steps. Netty was gone for the night, on her way home. Longarm still wasn't exactly sure how he felt about that.

He took a swallow of the whiskey Cathy Sue had poured for him a bit ago and puffed on the plump, pale cigar. She'd not only brought it to him, she'd also taken a candle and lighted it for him. He propped his feet up on the ottoman she'd set down before him and pretended to read the three-day-old *Rocky Mountain News* she'd spread in his lap.

About the only thing she'd missed bringing him for this domestic scene, he realized, was an old dog to curl up alongside his feet.

And that, it now occurred to him, just very well might be part of the reason why he wasn't so hot and eager to leap into the middle of Miss Cathy Sue Lark.

He *liked* her, for cryin' out loud. And he didn't want to abuse her. And more to the point, Cathy Sue was a sweet and special little bit of a thing, and her kind was more for marrying than for catch-as-catch-can slap an' tickle.

Custis Long, on the other hand, was not of a marrying inclination. Not the least lick tempted. Not even by a girl as sweet and dear as little Cathy Sue.

And that, by damn, was that. He would just set this glass aside—he did—and put the newspaper onto the table—he did—and take his feet down off the ottoman—he stood upright on his own hind legs—and just slide on out and . . .

"Hello, Cathy Sue." He smiled.

She smiled back at him. She was standing in the doorway.

And she hadn't come into the parlor to freshen his drink. That became clear pretty quick.

"Custis." She stepped forward, tiny and delicate and pretty as a picture, and looked up at him. He laid the pale cigar down in the ashtray she'd provided for him. He cleared his throat. Loudly. Twice. Really now, he oughtn't. . . .

Despite all his good intentions, Longarm found himself kissing the girl.

She was so light in his arms he couldn't be entirely sure she was real, but her mouth tasted faintly of raspberries and cream. He could get real fond of the flavor of raspberries and cream.

Cathy Sue wriggled a little, trying to get down, so he lowered her gently until her feet touched the floor again. Damned if he wasn't just a wee bit wobble-legged and horny too. He had a hard-on fit to bust buttons. This wasn't at *all* the way it was supposed to work.

"Cathy Sue, shouldn't we kinda . . . I mean . . ."

She was smiling at him. But not an ordinary cheerful sort of smile at all. This one was overheated and sexy.

She shrugged her shoulders and her dress—what'd happened to all those buttons anyhow?—slithered down to waist level.

Cathy Sue Lark had herself a figure after all. It wasn't much by dairy-cow proportions, but it was sure enough a genuine grown-up woman's figure. With tits and everything.

Her waist looked like he could reach all the way around it

and touch fingertips and thumb. With one hand.

Her titties were small but perky. Tiny little teacups with pale, pink miniature rosebuds at their tips.

Her belly was flat and her neck slim.

She pushed the dress down past the slight swell of her hips, and the garment fell into a loose circle around her feet.

Which he now noticed were already bare.

And somehow, sometime, somewhere she'd shed her underthings too. He was pretty sure she'd been wearing undergarments during supper. Surely he would've noticed otherwise. But they weren't with her now.

Now she was standing naked and cute, posing like she was some statue on a statehouse lawn.

Her hips were shapely and her legs slim almost to the point of being scrawny, yet somehow with a most alluring shape of their own.

Cathy Sue lifted her arms. She was still smiling. She blew a kiss to him and at the same time tugged some pins out of her hair.

Her hair dropped loose, flowing down over her shoulders, part of it onto her chest. She had a light sprinkling of freckles on the bony chest plate that was above and between her breasts, he noticed.

And now that he was paying attention he could see that she had a dusting of freckles across the bridge of her nose—had he ever noticed before how awful pretty her eyes were? not blue like he'd always thought but gray lightly flecked with gold—and a little bitty scar at the left corner of her mouth. Which was open just a little. And moist. Definitely moist. She licked her lips. And continued to smile that peculiar/particular way she'd lately taken to doing.

She was naked and she was lovely and if he had any damn sense at all he would sashay right out of there quick before . . .

She stepped forward so that she was immediately before him.

Without saying a word—she didn't actually have to if the truth be known—she dropped to her knees.

And reached up to commence unbuttoning his fly.

Longarm groaned. He shucked out of his coat and unbuckled his gunbelt, dropping the big Colt and holster into the chair behind him.

He heard a gasp and looked down. Cathy Sue had him out of the confinement of his trousers by now. She stroked and fondled the one-eyed snake for a moment.

Then she leaned forward.

Her breath on him was hot.

Her lips were even hotter.

And when she took him into her mouth, Longarm damn near lost all control. What little bit of it he had left.

He was weak in the knees, and when she pulled at him it seemed only right and natural to comply. He sat down, unmindful of the gunbelt that was pressing hard and cold against his butt. There were other things of pressing interest at the moment, and those were maybe hard but in no way cold.

"Cathy Sue, honey, are you sure you wanta . . ."

But hell, it was too late to talk about.

Cathy Sue sucked and smiled and fondled, and Custis Long wasn't in control of anything anymore. Not right at the time he wasn't.

He closed his eyes and this time it was his turn to gasp, and that cute little ol' Cathy Sue proved to him beyond question that she was a woman grown with a grown woman's ways as his pleasures grew and expanded and passed the point of containment so that everything exploded, rushing and gushing out of him and into her and *damn* but there was a lot to be said for cute little blondes that looked like alabaster figurines but with the heat and the savvy and the will deep down where it counted.

"Son of a *bitch* but you're good," he whispered when finally he had breath enough back to do so.

Cathy Sue let his momentarily limp—but still willing—member slide out of her mouth, and lifted her pretty face to give him another of those knowing, feline smiles. Then she winked and slowly, showing off about it, circled her mouth with the tip of her tongue to capture and take in a few lingering drops of sticky, milky fluid.

"Anything, Custis. I'd do *any*thing for you."

With a sigh of capitulation—what the hell else could a fella do—he reached down to take her by the arms and pull her into his lap where he could cuddle and pet her.

She'd told him before there was a lot she still didn't know.

Well, the way he saw it, she was the sort of girl he'd be proud and pleased to take on as a pupil.

And they had all the night long to study in.

Chapter 6

He tugged the cinch strap tight and reached up to fetch the stirrup off the horn and let it down—not dropping it but letting it down gently so as not to startle the horse—and then turned to hem and haw and scuff his toe through the dirt a little. He was feeling awkward and more than a little shy this morning.

"You, um, tell your daddy that I appreciate the use of this here horse that he don't know he's loaned me. You'll do that, won't you, Cathy Sue?"

"Custis. Why won't you look at me?"

He didn't answer her.

"Wasn't I good enough for you, Custis? Didn't I please you last night?"

"Dammit, Cathy Sue, you were wonderful. And you know it."

"I thought we were awfully good together, Custis. But that was last night. Now this morning you're acting like you're disappointed with me. Or ashamed of me or something."

"It ain't you I'm ashamed of. It's me and the way . . . dammit, Cathy Sue, your daddy has been a good friend t' me. Now look what I done. Come in here with him gone an' instead of taking care of his place in his absence, I up an' despoil his only daughter. Instead o' acting the friend I act the thief. If he was t' know he'd hate me sure. And he'd be right to. I oughtn't to of done those things with you last night, girl. I should've been stronger an' better than that. I knew better, an' the fault is on me for not doing what was right."

"Wallow in your own guilt if you want to, Custis Long, but I know what I know. And I know that what we had between us last night was wonderful. I'll keep the memory of it always, and no matter what else happens to me for the rest of my days, I'll be able to call on those memories whenever I want to think of something nice. And I know something else too, Custis Long. I know that I love you. No, don't look at me like that. I'm not trying to lay any claim against you. I'm just saying something that's true. I love you. I don't want t' marry you or tie you to me. Nothing like that. I just, in my own way, kinda love you. Now go on with whatever you come here t' do, Custis. I'll tell Papa you was here an' that you got Red Boy with you. When you're done with him, bring him back. I'll be here and I'll be loving you and if you want into my bed again, I'll open myself up to you then just like I did last night, because you can feel guilty 'bout it if you want, Custis, but what I feel right now is tingly and warm all over, like I could still feel your hands and your tongue all over me. You know?" She laughed. "You do. You can feel it too. I can see that in the way you're looking at me right this very minute, Custis. You liked last night as much as I did, and you'll be back for more the next chance you get. I hope. Now go on. Get out of here before I grab hold of you an' drag you onto the ground right here in the middle of the damn yard and the two of us are locked up like a pair of dogs in heat when my daddy or somebody rides in. Go on now, Custis. Git." She turned and walked away, back into the house with a slam of the screened door, without telling him good-bye and without again looking in his direction.

31

Longarm took a long, deep breath, let it out slowly, and then with a shake of his head swung onto the red horse's back. It was a ways to go yet to reach Palmer Lake, and his eye-opener this morning hadn't been either coffee or breakfast but a last-minute romp atop Cathy Sue's lithe and energetic little body.

He was still ashamed of himself. But only a very little bit now.

He whistled as he rode, and half an hour later he felt cheerful enough to tip his Stetson to the Larks' hired man, Benny, who was riding bleary-eyed and shaky in the opposite direction as he returned from a night in town.

Benny pretended to recognize him but didn't, which for some reason Longarm found to be amusing.

For one brief and ungenerous moment Longarm found himself wondering if the one name Cathy Sue had withheld from him when she'd spoken of her past lovers was Benny's. But naw, that couldn't be, he quickly assured himself. Give the girl credit for more sense than that. He winked at the blinking, uncomprehending cowboy, and trotted on in the direction of Palmer Lake, where he had several papers to serve. And near which Eudora M. Parks lived.

"Miz Parks?"

A man had to look close now to see that this aging and work-worn woman might once have had the bright, fresh beauty of youth.

Billy Vail's perceptions of the lady were no doubt colored by the past. And so they should be. But what Longarm saw was a woman to whom time had been unkind.

She was stooped and graying, her shoulders rounded with age and labor and her flesh hanging loose and liver-spotted. Her lips were thin and pressed tight together. Her mouth lay in the center of a network of tiny wrinkles that radiated out in all directions from that tight-puckered center. Dark satchels

32

big enough to pack picnic lunches in hung beneath her eyes, and wattles of sagging skin dangled off her chin and neck like dewlaps on an old and ugly cow.

But the eyes that looked back at him were bright and clear and so lovely that for a moment Longarm could almost see her as she'd been when she was a girl and Billy Vail was in love with her.

She'd been pretty then, he could see. Damn near beautiful with those eyes and those cheekbones and that small, delicate nose. He could see that for just an instant, and then the instant passed and she was an old and frightened woman once more.

"Who are you?" she demanded.

Longarm doffed his hat and tried his best to look harmless—no small trick that—and innocent—which was every bit as difficult to accomplish. "One of Marshal Vail's deputies, ma'am. I've come to see about the government livestock that was stolen from around here."

"The gov . . . oh, yes. That government livestock."

"Yes, ma'am."

"Come in then. I have a pot of tea on the stove, or I can make coffee if you won't take tea."

"Yes, ma'am. Thank you."

"Well don't just stand there, sonny. Come inside and shut that door quick before you let half the flies in Colorado in with you."

"Yes, ma'am."

Custis Long, chief deputy marshal for the Denver District, Attorney General's office, United States Justice Department, jumped to do as he was told.

Chapter 7

It was a pure marvel, that's what it was. How any human person could expect to support herself off of so little . . . well, it was an amazement, that was all. A marvel.

Mrs. Parks—she'd told him he could call her Eudora, but it just wasn't in him to be so casually informal with a woman of Mrs. Parks's age; when he was a boy something like that would have gotten his ears boxed for him, and those lessons were so deeply ingrained now that it would have been nigh impossible for him to ignore them even by invitation—survived off the production of eighteen milk cows.

Not even big cows, at that. What Longarm had expected to find on a dairy farm would be some of those crazy-colored spotted critters with the bony hips and the big udders. It seemed like those big, leggy German-bred cows were all the rage in dairying now, and no wonder since they ate no more than any other kind of cow, yet gave out so much milk the farmers claimed to need barrels underneath them instead of buckets to collect it all.

Mrs. Parks's cows were little bitty things with great, huge, soft brown eyes and eyelashes so long and curly they would turn a Denver debutante green with raw envy. They—the cows, not the debutantes—were shades of tan and khaki and tawny brown. They were pretty things. Prettier, in some ways, than a good many of the debutantes.

The cows were small enough they could have been taken in as house pets. All right, Longarm silently acknowledged, that was an exaggeration. But not much of one. The truth was that these little cows weren't at all what Billy Vail had led him to expect to see here.

"You don't recognize them?"

"No, ma'am. But then I've never claimed t' be much of a hand when it come to dairy stock, Miz Parks."

The old woman smiled and petted one of the pretty little things. The cow was pushing its nose through the fence rails in an effort to nuzzle Mrs. Parks's side. She moved closer so that it could reach her and gently scratched it behind the ears. The cow looked like it was going to pass out from sheer contentment, Longarm thought. "They are jerseys," Mrs. Parks said. "One of the Channel Islands breeds."

"Yes, ma'am." The response was a matter of politeness, not comprehension. Longarm had no idea what she was talking about. As far as he knew a jersey was a kind of shirt. And it wasn't made of leather either. As for some islands that he'd never heard of, well . . .

"They are wonderful creatures really. A little tender, and I have to keep them sheltered when the weather is too bad. But I've never known any animals nicer than my jerseys. They are wonderful companions. They are good keepers too and give an amazing return. Really quite something for their size."

"Yes, ma'am." Longarm, though, was frowning. Things would have been much easier from his point of view if the lady had those black and white patchy-coated things. A holstein's hide stands out in a crowd, and if someone was stealing the lady's steers to have one to butcher now and then, the skin would make for easily identifiable evidence of the fact. But these jerseys, aside from being smaller, had hides that pretty much looked like longhorns', just not so freckled and speckled. The skin off one of these cows could be thrown onto a pile of longhorn hides and no one would ever notice.

"I have my milkers on a two-year breeding rotation," Mrs. Parks rambled on. "Nine calves per year that comes to. Since there isn't any jersey bull close—I buy my heifers from a gentleman in Florence—I have to settle for crossbreeding just to keep my girls producing, you see. I use a neighbor's Texas bull for that. Very small calves that old-time breed produces. Not so big that the calves would hurt my jerseys, which one of the new beef breeds could do. But those Texas cows give very little milk. You couldn't possibly use one of them for dairy purposes. That means all my calves are surplus, not only the males. Male or female, I raise them all to sell for meat. Nine each year." She sighed heavily.

"I count on those sales, Marshal Long, I surely do. Milk and butter only bring me so much of a cash return. I need the money from selling my calves too. And you can see in that pasture right there how many I have left. The nine babies from this year and now only three yearlings from last year's calf crop. Three left, and I've only sold two. Four have been stolen, sir. If the rest go too . . ." She was crying a little now, the tears coursing down her wrinkled cheeks, although she was able to keep her voice fairly steady. "I simply do not know what I shall have to do. I haven't the strength to tend any more of a garden than I already do. As it is it's all I can do to feed and milk my girls and keep up with the house garden. And I don't know where I could cut back on spending. I only buy a little salt and flour and like that. I drink milk and herb teas that I pick and dry myself. I only keep a bit of coffee on hand for company. Most of what I make has to be paid out for taxes and other such necessaries. I just don't know what else . . . oh, dear. I'm nattering, aren't I? My late husband Roy always did say that I talk much too much. Am I talking too much, Marshal Long?"

He smiled. "You're doing just fine, Mrs. Parks. Let's go back inside for one more cup of that good tea, then I'll take another look around out here and see what I can see."

"You are very kind, Marshal. Thank you."

"My pleasure, ma'am." He offered his arm and began escorting her back toward the house.

"Could I . . . would you mind . . ."

"Ma'am?"

"Would you talk to me about William? It is wicked of me, I know, but I would like to hear about him. How he lives. What folks in the capital think of him. Anything you would care to tell me."

Longarm patted the thin and bony fingers that had a surprisingly firm grip on his forearm—perhaps not so surprising when he recalled that those age-worn hands still managed to milk eighteen cows twice each day every day of the whole long year—and said, "Why, ma'am, we'll have us a nice long talk this afternoon, and I'll tell you anything you want t' know about the marshal."

Chapter 8

Palmer Lake was a community that catered to the needs, the wants, and the pocketbooks of visitors from elsewhere.

Lodges and boardinghouses dotted the hillsides and covered pavilions lined the lakeshore.

Visitors would come from miles away to stay for a week or two in accommodations ranging from the rustic to the elegant.

Hundreds more poured in for short day visits. Special trains ran from Denver bringing families, fraternal organizations, church groups, and what-have-you to picnic and take the sun or the waters.

There was no direct rail service to the lake resort community, so passengers for Palmer Lake disembarked at the Monument depot and were transported the few additional miles by fleets of commodious coaches.

Unlike most such areas, at least most in Longarm's experience, Palmer Lake catered to the desires of all classes and kinds of folks. The wealthy were welcome here—as they were anywhere—but so were the working classes.

Among the customers lined up at the ice cream kiosk or gathered beneath the roofs of adjoining picnic shelters a rich merchant and his pampered daughters might be side by side with a loudly enthusiastic family of Italian immigrants, their baskets overflowing with hard breads and redolent cheeses.

Longarm liked Palmer Lake. But he did not know it well. It was not the sort of community where his particular services would often be needed.

Still, every place had its share of lawbreakers, and Palmer Lake was no exception. The sheriff of El Paso County had a deputy in the town to handle the needs of the northern part of his jurisdiction. Longarm looked the man up as soon as he reached town, in the waning hours of the afternoon.

"Deputy Vance?"

The deputy, a thin man with gray hair and not much of it, removed his spectacles and laid a newspaper carefully aside before he responded. "It's Deputy Hollowell actually. Vance Hollowell. What can I do for you?"

Longarm apologized for the misunderstanding and introduced himself. The deputy's expression brightened into a considerably warmer welcome than before. "Long. I've heard of you. All good, I might add."

Longarm grinned. "Shows you can't believe everything you hear."

Hollowell laughed and extended his hand for a shake. "No need for modesty here, Long."

"My friends call me Longarm, Deputy." He winked and added, "So do some folks I don't much care for, but we won't get into that."

"Fine, Longarm, if you'll drop the formalities with me too. Now let me ask it again. What brings you to my peaceful little part of the world, and how can I help you with whatever business you have?"

"Routine service of some papers, Vance, and one minor investigation. Theft o' government property, some cows that were on land owned by a Mrs. E. M. Parks. You might know the lady. She lives a few miles northeast from here."

"I know Mrs. Parks, of course. Not well. She doesn't come

to town all that often. Nice lady, though, from what I do know of her. You say she had some of Uncle Sam's cows on her place? I didn't know she had land enough to rent pasture to the government."

"These were some of her own stock that she'd donated to the Bureau of Indian Affairs. Some sort of charity thing, I suppose. Point is, she'd donated these steers to the government an' transferred title, then they came up missing before anybody got around t' picking them up. That makes it our loss an' brings me into the thing. I'm sure not trying to step on your toes, Vance."

"I never thought you were, Longarm." Hollowell rubbed his neck and shivered a little like he was trying to shake off a chill. The man did not look well, and Longarm wondered if perhaps he had been sent up here to Palmer Lake to serve out time enough for retirement in peace and quiet. "I recall Mrs. Parks making out a complaint—that was before I came up here, but there is a report on it in the files Johnny left me—something about two of her steers being missing."

"Recent?" Longarm asked.

"I don't recall exactly when this would have been. I've been here a little more than a month. It was before that sometime, of course. I can look up the dates if you need to know."

"I don't think that'll be necessary. Interesting, though, t' hear this is a continuing problem then, what with her losin' other stock before," Longarm said, as if he hadn't known that already. "Do your reports say what this Johnny fella did for her?"

"Oh, I don't have to read through them again to tell you that, Longarm. Mrs. Parks was told she needed to file her complaint with Douglas County. That's where the theft took place, you see."

"Oh?"

"Mrs. Parks lives close to us as the nearest town, but we're in El Paso County here and her place is across the line in Douglas County. I'm sure of that, Longarm. And that's what Johnny wrote down in his report that he told her to do. To file her complaint up there. It's a shame we couldn't help. I know Johnny wanted to. So would I. Like I said, she seems a real nice lady. I wish there was something we could do for her. But you know how it is."

"Yes, of course." Longarm pulled out a pair of cheroots and offered one of them to Vance Hollowell, then struck a lucifer and lighted both smokes.

"Now that's what I call a nice smoke," the deputy said appreciatively.

"Glad you like it. D'you know if the lady did anything about pursuing that other complaint then, Vance? I mean, if somebody's already plowed this ground I'd sure rather glean off his rows than break new sod o' my own."

"Wish I could tell you, Longarm, but I just don't know about that. You'd have to ask the boys up in Castle Rock. There isn't a Douglas County deputy assigned permanent in the south part of the county. Not that I know of, anyhow. Practically no people in southeastern Douglas, you see. Just a few ranches and like that, but no towns and not hardly any need for a lawman. No, you'd have to ask in Castle Rock. Wish I could help you with it."

Longarm shrugged and reached inside his coat to pull out the thin sheaf of documents he'd been given earlier. "About these warrants and subpoenas, Vance. I could use some help locating the fellas named on 'em." The court papers were real, not just a cover to give him an excuse to be in the neighborhood so he could help Billy Vail's friend Eudora. Leave it to Henry to slip that extra bit of effort in.

"Now that," Hollowell said, "I should be able to do something about. Let me see who all you have here." He leaned forward and reached for the papers Longarm extended to him.

Chapter 9

"These two," Hollowell said, keeping a pair of the documents and returning the rest to Longarm. "I can help you with these two. This here one, Jess Youngmeir, he has a little truck farm a couple miles out of town. Late as it is you probably won't want to go out there till tomorrow, but I can give you directions easy enough. You can't miss Jess's place. Then this guy, Leonard Morgan, he lives right here in town. Not a bad fella. I know right where you can find him. What I'd suggest, Longarm, is that you and me go over there to the Cork and Copper—that's where Len stops for a beer or two most every evening after work—and we'll have a little something for the stomach ourselves while we're there. Afterward you come with me over to the house—the Cork and Copper is as good as on the way—and take supper with me and my missus."

"Now that's what I call a fine an' generous offer, Vance," Longarm said.

"Glad to help a fellow officer any way I can." He chuckled. "Besides, if we have company at the table Dolly won't be doing any fussing at me for having some beers on the way home. Fine woman my Dolly, but she went to one of those Temperance Society meetings last year and has been a tad off her nut ever since. Used to enjoy wine as well as anyone, but not any longer. Doesn't want any of that Demon Rum—hell, Longarm, I don't like rum, never developed a taste for it, but she says it's all rum, even wine and beer—beneath her roof. Doesn't count that it's my roof too, she don't want no rum underneath it whoever it belongs to."

"Well, I'm always proud t' serve as a bad example for any man," Longarm said with a grin.

"Then by all means let's go serve a paper. And gain a tipple." The county deputy rose, placing his weight gingerly on one leg and reaching for a stout cane that Longarm hadn't noticed before.

The cane was quite obviously necessary for functional and not cosmetic purposes. Hollowell leaned heavily on it for support, using the cane in his left hand to lend assistance to a weak and shrunken right leg. Now that the man was standing and moving about Longarm could see that his right thigh was thin and wasted away in comparison with the left. But at least the cane allowed him free use of his right hand. And of the gun that was holstered at his waist there.

"In case you're wondering . . ." Hollowell began.

"I am," Longarm admitted.

"I used to be chief deputy for Sheriff Crowe. Then last winter a young buck—never mind what his name was, he was only appointed a deputy to make his daddy happy—him and me lucked into the middle of a bank robbery in Colorado City. You know the town?"

"I do."

"Salty place. I've always liked it. Didn't that day, though, let me tell you. Me and this boy should of had things under control, but the kid got scared and let off a shot when there wasn't need, and of course that scared the robbers so that they shot back, and next thing you knew there was hell to pay. Mind that step, Longarm, the board's loose." Hollowell closed the office door behind him, but did not bother to lock it even though there was a rack of rifles and shotguns inside. Peaceful kind of town, Longarm thought.

"Where was I. Oh, yes. Gunsmoke and lead all over the damn place. The kid who'd gone and started it all came out unhurt, naturally, but two of the robbers and one innocent customer were killed. And I near about lost this here leg to blood poisoning afterward. Funny thing. That was the third time I'd been shot in the line of duty. And every one of them hit me somewhere on this thigh, though never so bad before as that time at the bank. Anyway, I can get around now but not so spry as I ought. So the sheriff, he sent me up here so Dolly and me can take things easy until I qualify for my pension. Two years, three months, and, uh, about a week and a half to go." Hollowell's smile flashed. "More or less."

Longarm laughed. But he did not for one moment believe that Vance Hollowell was looking forward to retirement. This was a man who would much rather remain in harness.

"That's the Cork and Copper across the street there, Longarm. Mind you don't trip in the ruts now. We ought to drag these streets more often what with all the wheeled traffic we have in and out, but the town hasn't the budget for it and the problem isn't quite bad enough for the merchants to get together on their own to handle it."

"I'll try an' not fall down, thank you."

Hollowell gave him an odd look, then realized Longarm was pulling his leg—the good one, presumably—and guffawed.

The Cork and Copper turned out to be a small and comfortable little neighborhood saloon, the sort of place frequented by locals and unnoticed by the tourists.

"H'lo, Vance, haven't seen you for a while."

"Hello yourself, Burt. This is my friend Marshal Long out of Denver. He's a very important man, Burt, but his money is no good in here. These are on me."

"Now Vance," Longarm protested.

"No, I insist. It's my pleasure. Really."

"Burt, tell him he isn't being fair."

"Don't ask me to get into the middle of this, Marshal. Besides, I got no choice about it. You're passing through. Vance I got to live with. And he's mean, he is. If I crossed him and took money from you, Marshal, Vance would find me in violation of some county regulation or other and have me in the pokey in no time. No, sir, I can't risk that. Not no way." The bartender was grinning when he said all that. He was also very efficiently drawing a pair of beers and placing them on the bar, and while he was at it slid a bowl of nuts close and spun the free-lunch platter so that the freshest and nicest bits of ham and pickle and whatnot were toward Deputy Hollowell. The deputy, Longarm decided, was much liked in his newly adopted community. That spoke volumes about him and all of it favorable.

Hollowell saluted Longarm with an upraised mug, then took a deep swallow that he followed with a belch and a smile. "Now that's fittin', Burt."

"Thankyuhthankyuh."

"Has Leonard been in yet this evening?"

"Morgan?"

"Uh, huh."

"No, but I look for him any time now. Shorty Bemis broke some spokes and darn near wrecked his coach this forenoon, so I expect Len's been extra busy at fixing the wheel. That work isn't real easy, kinda tedious and delicate, so I don't wonder that he'd be taking his time with it."

Hollowell nodded, and for Longarm's benefit explained, "Your man Morgan works for Carter Brouiard's outfit. They run transfer and excursion coaches for the out-of-towners. Len is in charge of maintenance on all the coaches and the harness and the like, everything except the livestock."

"I see."

"Len isn't in any trouble, is he?" Burt asked, obviously looking for gossip to spread.

"Just a routine court appearance," Longarm said, "and just as a witness at that. He hasn't done anything himself."

Burt tried not to look disappointed.

"Don't fill up on this free lunch," Vance advised, reaching for a pickled egg, "or Dolly will get her feelings hurt. She's a fine hand in the kitchen and likes to see folks dig deep into the serving bowls."

Longarm, who hadn't yet taken anything off the lunch platter, nodded and downed the rest of his beer.

"Another round, gents?" Burt asked.

"One more time," Hollowell told him.

"Coming right up, and . . . hey!" The bartender looked across the room, an impish grin playing on his thin face of a sudden. "Better watch yourself, Len. There's a Ewe Ess deppity marshal here a-lookin' for you."

He was only being playful. Longarm knew that. The man never would have said anything if he'd thought there was anything remotely serious about Longarm's interest in Leonard Morgan.

Longarm understood all that.

The fact remained.

Burt was dumb as a root hog carved out of moldy shit.

A tall, middle-aged man who'd just entered the saloon froze in mid-stride, quick fear wiping all expression from his face and draining his complexion of color so that the stubble of a heavy beard showed starkly black against the pallor of his skin.

"Oh, Jesus!" he moaned.

"Hey, it's all right," Longarm tried to tell him.

But too late.

Len Morgan, wanted for no more than an appearance in court to testify about a simple trespass, reached into a pocket of his greasy coveralls and pulled out a shiny, palm-sized Smith and Wesson break-top revolver.

"Don't . . ."

Longarm tried to retrieve the situation, but Vance Hollowell was standing between him and Morgan, and Hollowell was moving too, his pistol coming up fast. As he drew, though, he tried to drop into a pistoleer's crouch and lost his balance on his weak right side, sending him lurching into Longarm's shoulder and throwing Longarm out of the way.

The little Smith snapped and spat.

Vance Hollowell cried out and went down.

With a curse under his breath Longarm leveled his Colt and triggered a slug into Len Morgan's breastbone.

It was *not* what he wanted to do, dammit. But what choice did he have?

Morgan dropped his revolver and toppled face-forward into the sawdust on the floor.

By then Longarm was already kneeling at Vance Hollowell's side.

"You're gonna be all right, friend."

Hollowell was as pale now as Morgan had just been.

"Is it . . . what I think?"

"I'm afraid so."

"Shit."

Deputy Hollowell had been shot, naturally enough, in the right thigh.

"The sheriff isn't gonna believe this. Neither will Dolly, damn it."

"It isn't a bad one, though, Vance. You're going to be just fine. You'll need a little time t' heal, that's all."

"And Len?"

"Wish I could say the same 'bout him."

"Damn," Hollowell complained.

"Yeah."

47

Both men gave Burt a sour look. The bartender winced and turned away.

A few paces distant some of the other customers were tending to Morgan. Or trying to.

"He's dead, I'm feared," one of them said. Longarm had already known that from the limp, unprotected way the man's body hit the floor. Morgan was dead before he had time enough to bounce.

"Anybody know what the hell that was all about?" someone else asked.

"Nope. Something somewhere in his past that he felt guilty about," Longarm guessed. "Could be we'll figure out what it was, but more likely we never will know. He heard he was wanted and came up shooting. It happens like that sometimes, sad t' say. Give me that towel there, Burt. We need t' get something wrapped tight around Deputy Hollowell's leg here. And d'you have a good doctor in town?"

"Plenty o' doctors here, mister. They get a lot o' business off the out-o'-towners."

"You'd best bring one then. A good one. The deputy needs some looking after. Oh, and somebody go tell his wife he'll be late for supper tonight."

"I'll go. You want I should tell her why he's late?"

"Gawd, no," Hollowell blurted out.

The men Longarm pointed to took off on their various errands, and soon things were more or less back to normal at the Cork and Copper. Except for the county deputy lying on the floor with a small-caliber bullet in his thigh and one of the local craftsmen lying dead a few yards away.

"Remind me t' get a copy of the death certificate," Longarm said. "The judge will want that so he can vacate this subpoena. He's a stickler for the little details, this one."

"That will be the first thing on my mind all evening, Longarm," Hollowell said. "Meantime, why don't you hand

48

me down that beer to where I can reach it. And maybe something off the lunch plate too. I swear I'm starved half to death, and what Dolly don't know can't hurt me."

Longarm smiled and moved to do as the wounded man asked. "I tell you, Vance. Now that the sheriff has moved you up here to where it's so peaceful and quiet, you're likely t' wind up fat an' lazy, what with having no lawing to do or anything."

"Ain't that the truth. But Longarm?"

"Yeah."

"Tomorrow morning when you go out to serve paper on that vegetable farmer?"

"Yes."

"If it's all the same to you, Longarm, I think I'm gonna be too busy to go along."

Longarm chuckled a little, and reached for a bite-sized chunk of smoked sausage off the lunch platter he was offering to Hollowell.

Beneath that surface, though, his thoughts were . . . not dark . . . saddened. That was it, he decided. Just so very damn sad. Such a waste, Leonard Morgan's death had been. Such a damned stupid waste.

"You. Move aside there, mister. Let me get to my patient."

"Whatever you say, Doc." Longarm made room for the doctor.

Pain and blood and dying. And not a bit of it necessary. Shit.

Longarm replaced the lunch platter on the bar and stepped well out of the way. The least he could do would be to stay until the doctor was through and then help Hollowell home.

Longarm only wished he could do as much for Morgan, but a man in sleeve garters and a dirty shirt came in and directed the removal of the body.

Shit, Longarm thought again.

Chapter 10

He used a pinch of soft, fluffy biscuit to mop up the last bit of rich gravy, then leaned back with a sigh. "No, ma'am, I couldn't hold another bite. Really." The woman clucked her disapproval, but did consent to take her skillet back to the range.

"Your wife is quite a cook, Jess. Reckon if I was your hired hand I'd plump up like a goose before Christmas. Thanks."

"Our pleasure, Long. You should come by on a Sunday sometime."

Longarm smiled. "Don't tempt me or I just might."

"I wasn't just a-talkin'," Jess Youngmeir insisted. "I meant it. You drop by any Sunday. There'll be a place at the table for you."

"I just might could do that too. Thank you." Longarm stifled a belch and carefully folded his napkin before placing it beside his near-spotless plate. "One thing I got to say, Jess. It ain't everybody I serve papers on that turns out t' be so friendly an' fine a fella as you. And o' course your missus here too. Believe me, it's been a real pleasure meetin' you folks."

"Our pleasure, Long. As for that subpoena," Youngmeir said with a shrug, "I figure all I have to do is show up when they want an' tell the truth to whatever they ask me. I see no harm in that."

"Sounds like you have a clearer conscience than most of the men I deal with," Longarm observed.

"There's no trick to it," Youngmeir said. "Just do what you think is right an' don't lie about it afterward. Seems to me that's a right fair way to get along, even if a fella does make a mistake now an' then."

"I wish everybody did like that, Jess. My job would sure be easier for it."

"I'll do what I can to make it so, Long, and you do the same. One person at a time. That's all any of us can be responsible for, just ourselves. If we each try an' do that, maybe someday it'll all come together."

"I hope so," Longarm said.

"One more cup of coffee, Marshal? It's still hot," Mrs. Youngmeir suggested.

"Thank you, ma'am, but reckon I'd best pass, good though it is. I got a long ways t' go yet today." Longarm thanked the lady of the house again and went outside, Jess Youngmeir trailing companionably along with him while Mrs. Youngmeir started in on the dishes.

"Mind now," Longarm said. "The sixteenth o' next month. In the Federal Building up t' Denver. Second floor. Ask for John Wixler an' tell him you're a friend o' mine. He's the bailiff for Judge Adamle, and he'll see you're comfortable."

"That's fine of you, Long, thanks."

"The least I could do after you an' the missus been so nice t' me here this morning." He snugged the cinch on the borrowed horse and let the stirrup down. "Could I ask one more thing of you before I go, Jess?"

"Certainly."

"This next fella I got to see is . . . I forget his name. Got it written down somewhere." That was not entirely true, although of course he had the name written down on the document he was to serve. It was just that Longarm was not in the habit of bandying about information that should best be kept private. And not everyone would appreciate strangers knowing he was being served court papers. "Anyway, he works at some outfit called the Rafter W. D'you know of it?"

"Lord, I hope so. That's the brand run by Senator Walker in Douglas County. The spread covers parts of Elbert and El Paso Counties too, I think."

"I've heard o' Walker o' course."

"Anybody who can read knows about the senator, I would think. And anyone who can hear. The senator is big on making speeches."

"He's big on most everything the way I hear it."

"You got that 'un right. You want me to tell you how to get to the Rafter W?"

"I'd appreciate it."

Youngmeir gave simple, concise directions that were so clear Longarm thought they might even be accurate. Quite often a person found himself sent off in strange directions by well-intentioned folks, but Jess Youngmeir seemed to know what he was saying.

Longarm heard him out, then turned as if to mount, stopping at the last moment and casually asking, "Oh, by the by. D'you know a Mrs. Parks? She lives a little way north an' east from here."

"Eudora? Sure we do. My Bessie counts Eudora a good friend. They're both of 'em on the church committee to visit shut-ins, do their quilting together, go out every year to gather wild plums for making jam. You bet we know Eudora. Salt of the earth is what she is. Anybody around here would tell you that, Long."

"I don't suppose you know anything about some steers o' hers that went missing."

52

"Only that she's had some losses. Naturally I did hear about that."

"Any ideas about who might've taken them?"

"Losing one animal at a time like that, you kinda have to think it's somebody helping himself to some meat, not somebody stealing for profit. Be real hard to find somebody like that, I'd think, since most everybody around here raises a little meat an' butchers for himself. Tell you what, though. If I hear any whispers or anybody goes to bragging on himself, I'll sure pass the word along."

"To me if I'm still around, or else you could tell Deputy Hollowell. I'd be grateful for the help."

"Count on it. If I hear anything, I'll sure let you know."

"It's been a real pleasure meeting you, Jess."

"Same here."

The two men shook, and Longarm swung onto his saddle.

It was true what he'd told Jess Youngmeir. The world would be a whole lot happier if more men were like Jess.

Longarm touched a finger to the brim of his Stetson in salute, then bumped the horse into a lope. He had some ground to cover before dark and the journey wouldn't get any shorter by sitting there thinking about it.

The red horse with John Lark's brand on its near shoulder moved along at a rocking-chair gait, putting the dusty miles behind.

Chapter 11

Jess Youngmeir's directions were as good as Longarm could have hoped. He reached the Rafter W in the hot, waning hours of the afternoon.

The ranch headquarters was an impressive sprawl of buildings large, small, and in between.

The main house was huge. And so newly completed there still was paint on the ground in the flower beds around it. Longarm doubted the workmen had been gone more than a few weeks after finishing the construction. It had two full floors above ground, plus a dormer in the attic space and a basement underneath. Porches surrounded it on three sides at ground level, and there were matching balconies with ornamental balustrades above the colonnaded porches. Stained-glass fanlights were set above the front door, and brightly polished brass coach lamps were mounted along the outside walls. There were windows beyond counting, and a brass chandelier hung over the main entry too. At night, when it was all lit up, the place most likely looked like a fairy castle, Longarm figured.

Really it was quite the grand manor. Especially for something set out here in the middle of the grassy-grass where there wasn't anything else to catch the eye save low clouds and distant mesas.

The Rafter W was far enough to the east and the contours of the ground were such that the Front Range mountains could not be seen, although they weren't more than thirty or so miles away.

The rest of the place was nowhere near so new or so grand, although the rest of the buildings were all well made and sensible.

But then the rest of the place was devoted, obviously, to serious work. The big house was a showpiece for the senator and all his ambitions. It took no genius to see that.

Longarm pulled up at a water trough near one of the older buildings, and called out a hallo to anyone who wanted to listen. Politeness made him refrain from dismounting without an invitation to do so.

While he waited he looked around.

He could see the half-dugout soddy that more than likely had been the first house on the ranch. Now it probably was being used as a root cellar or for other dry storage.

There was a log house that had been added onto several times over the years. Longarm suspected that would have been where the senator lived until the big house was recently finished. Now the former main house likely would become the foreman's home.

There were two long, low structures that Longarm took to be a kitchen/grub hall and a bunkhouse.

There were equipment sheds, an icehouse, a smithy, a henhouse, corrals and sorting chutes, a house garden, a storehouse. . . . What there didn't seem to be much of was folks.

But then this was a working outfit, and working hands properly shouldn't be anywhere near roofs and walls in daylight. Anyone knew that.

"Hallo," Longarm called again.

A door slammed, and a man came out of the building Longarm thought was the kitchen and grub hall. "Keep your drawers on, dammit, I heard ye the first time."

"Howdy," Longarm said.

"Howdy yerself. Well don't just set there. Light down an' make yerself useful. You can bring me a bucket o' water after you tend t' that horse. Put 'im in that pen yonder. Hay's under that tarp, as any fool might plainly see. Help yourself. Grain's in that shed there, inside them tin-lined bins. Take all you want t' feed, but mind you, close the lid tight when you're done. We don't want no rats gettin' inta the oats. Soon as you're done with that, mister, you can fill the reservoir on my range an' fill the tank over my sink too. You'll see it plain enough. The well is out behind that shed there. If you're so blind you can't see it, then you got no business bein' here by yourself. Once you done those things you can wash up an' take it easy. I won't ask no more of you than that. Supper's a half hour past full dark. Anybody misses the first go-round don't eat till morning. Any questions?"

Longarm grinned. "No, sir. Nothing that won't wait until later."

"All right then. Be gettin' on with it."

"Right away." Longarm chuckled and set about his chores in the order set down by the bossy old cook.

Longarm leaned back against the rough logs of the cookhouse wall. He had his legs sprawled out and a cheroot between his teeth, and felt pretty much at peace with the world. It was coming sundown, and the Rafter W hands were beginning to drift in to the home place.

He hadn't asked how many hands George Walker was carrying at the moment, but judging from the long table laid out inside there would be over a dozen of them.

The smells coming from Leroy's kitchen—Longarm hadn't been given the man's last name and wouldn't have thought of asking—were enough to make his mouth water in anticipation.

A rider came by on his way to the corrals and stopped long enough to lean down and offer his hand. "I'm Brent, the foreman. If you're looking for work, neighbor, I got to tell you we're full up at the moment. But of course you're welcome to stay the night and start off with your belly full come morning."

"Thanks, but it isn't work I'm looking for." Longarm stood and introduced himself. After the ugly experience back in Palmer Lake he was extra careful to point out that his business here wasn't anything serious. "It's just a simple subpoena. Your man hasn't done anything wrong. The U.S. Attorney just wants t'ask Gerald Wood if he knows anything about a case they're prosecuting. They'll talk to him first with just the lawyers there. After that they'll decide do they want t' bring him back t' testify during the trial. If there's a trial, that is. Either way, he ain't in any trouble. The government will pay mileage for his travel and a day rate for his time. Neither him nor you oughta be out anything."

"Sounds fair to me, Marshal." Brent stood in his stirrups and swiveled around to stare off toward the south, although it was becoming too dark by now to see much of anything that wasn't awfully close. Over at the big house all the lamps were being lighted, the spectacle being every bit as impressive in the dusk as Longarm had expected. "Him and Tom Boone been checking the mud holes today lookin' for bogged critters. They shouldn't be long."

"No hurry," Longarm assured him. He smiled. "Considering the smells comin' outta Leroy's kitchen I'm in no mood t' hurry."

"You won't be sorry you waited, Marshal. The senator feeds real good."

"That's important, I know."

"You bet it is. If you'll excuse me now, Marshal?"

"Sure thing, Brent."

"See you later then." Instead of heading for the corrals, though, which was where he'd been going when he swung aside to greet the stranger, the Rafter W foreman reined his mount back in the direction of the main house and trotted briskly to it, dismounting there and going inside.

When he came out a few minutes later he stepped onto his saddle to ride the sixty or so yards back to the cookhouse, and once more stopped beside Longarm.

"I told the senator and Miss Gayle that you were here, Marshal. Hope you don't mind, but they said you should be their guest for dinner."

"What about . . . ?"

"The senator said he'd send word to me when dinner is over and you gentlemen are ready to have your cigars. Then I'm to fetch Gerald with me and come to the senator's office. You can have your talk with him there and do whatever it is you have to do. Oh, yes, if you've already carried your things into the bunkhouse, let me know. I'll have 'em brought over to you. The senator said you're to be their guest in the house overnight too."

Longarm sighed. He really would have preferred the rough pleasures of the bunkhouse to the starched surroundings of the big house.

But this looked like one of those occasions when he'd best serve Billy Vail's interests by putting on his most polite face and being mannerly and nice.

He reckoned he could manage that for one evening without it killing him.

Chapter 12

Custis Long was not easily surprised. George Walker managed it.

"No need to introduce yourself, Long, we've met before."

"Sir?"

"At the governor's Birthday Ball if I remember correctly. February of last year that would have been. You were there with . . . don't tell me . . . oh yes, of course; you were there with Theo Cloy's niece Isabelle. Marshal Vail introduced us. I remember it quite well because my late wife remarked what a dashing fellow you were and how smitten Isabelle seemed that evening." The senator was smiling.

And well he might. Phenomenal powers of memory were a stock-in-trade of the more gifted politician. But Longarm was impressed nonetheless. The evening had been long ago and the meeting brief.

Now that the senator was providing the reminders, though, Longarm could call back a memory or two of his own. About Isabelle Cloy Reardon—better not to think about her unless he was in private or he might embarrass himself with a bulge in his britches—and about the senator's wife too. That had been, what, about a year and a half ago, and the woman had been in poor health at the time. She'd died since. This past spring, Longarm thought, but of course he did not ask. And now the senator was affianced to a woman probably a third his age.

Longarm turned his attention from the senator to his lady-to-be—not a difficult transition to manage—and bowed low.

Miss Lillith Gayle curtsied in return and batted her eyelashes right furiously.

Oh, she was a charmer, this one. And handsome too. She had hair as sleek and glossy black as a bear cub's pelt and a complexion pale as bone china. The contrast was startling.

Her eyes were a bright and dancing blue, and her cheeks were apple-rounded and highlighted with dimples so darling they looked unreal.

Her waist was impossibly small—some women, Longarm had heard, underwent surgical removal of their lower ribs so they could fit into the smallest possible corsets; he had to wonder if Miss Gayle had done that—and her bosom jutted high and proud in another alluring contrast of extremes.

A flowing gown hid the rest of her physical attributes, but Longarm felt it safe to assume the lady would be perfection from tip to toenails.

She was, he judged, no more than twenty-and-a-bit, while the senator would be into his sixties or better.

The senator, Longarm thought, looked like one *very* happy fellow.

"Ma'am," Longarm said, almost but not quite brushing the back of her hand with his lips.

"Sir." Her smile was dizzying. No wonder the senator was so damn happy.

"Deputy Long's nickname is Longarm, my dear," the senator put in. "As in Long Arm of the law, ha, ha. That is right, isn't it, deputy?"

"Yes, sir, it is."

"They say you're the best."

"They, sir?"

The politician smiled and winked. "You wouldn't have me betray confidences, would you?"

"Not with witnesses around to overhear, no, sir."

Senator Walker roared his approval of that one, then clapped Longarm on the shoulder and guided him deeper into the house. "Come along, son. I'm sure you're hungry. And I know I am. Come along and let's enjoy our meal before we have to tend to the business that brought you here. And I must say it is always nice to have a new voice at the table, what? Very much our pleasure to have you here. Very much so."

Longarm allowed himself to be led where the senator wished, Miss Gayle trailing close behind.

"That was really something, sir. Thank you. And thank you, Miss Gayle. Everything was nice as it could be." Longarm dabbed at his mouth with a napkin that smelled of sunlight, then carefully laid it beside his plate.

The meal really had been something. A bit long on fancy, perhaps, and a trifle short on substance. But it was no lie to say that it'd been really something.

There'd been lamb chops with fussy little curly-paper pants on the bone ends—so a fella could pick 'em up and gnaw the bones without getting his fingers greasy? maybe, but Longarm hadn't felt up to trying out that theory—and some side dishes—Longarm hadn't yet figured out what they were—and some odd-looking noodles in a lumpy, green-tinged sauce that looked like it was spoiled but that didn't taste anything like it looked. Dessert had been a spoon-sized dab of custard with a warm syrup drizzled over it.

Really something, all right. And if Longarm was still hungry, well, that was the price of elegance. He supposed.

"Shall we retire to my office, Longarm? I have a box of Havanas I think you will like."

"Must you, dear?" Miss Gayle protested. "You know I have no objection to a little smoke, and I would certainly welcome the company."

"I wish we could stay, dear, but Longarm has official business he must tend to, you know."

Miss Gayle made a pouting, petulant face.

"Now, now, darling. It is necessary. Besides, Longarm's business involves one of the hired men. Better we don't bring it into the dining room, eh?"

"Whatever you say, Georgie-bear, but I shall want to know everything that is said. I've never seen a deputy arrest anyone before. Promise me."

The senator laughed. "It will be nothing so dramatic as all that, love."

"Promise me anyway."

"Very well, my dear. I promise."

Mollified, Miss Gayle tilted her pretty head to offer her cheek for the senator to kiss. Longarm wasn't given that privilege, but he did get a bright and cheerful smile before Walker led him out of the huge dining room and off to the other side of the house to a wood-paneled and decidedly masculine study/den/office retreat.

Carl Brent, the foreman, and Gerald Wood, the cowboy whose testimony was wanted in Denver, were already waiting there.

The senator, Longarm saw, was a man who could change his stripes to meet his surroundings. At dinner he had been the attentive swain paying court to her ladyship. In the capital he was the consummate politician playing promise against rumor for advantage and power. Here in this room George Walker was a cowman presiding with knowledge and genial goodwill over men who were his employees but not his underlings. Here he was—or played at being—among his equals.

"So, boys," the senator said cheerfully. "Let's break out the liquor and have us a pull before we get bogged down in any serious shit. Longarm, set yourself down over there. Gerald, why don't you help yourself to a stogie outa that box there and pass the rest around. Brent, you know where I hide the good bottle. And I'll fetch the glasses. We'll all have a snort, and then you boys can take care of your business. Soon as that's done I'd like a rundown on the state of the graze and how the water's holding up. From you too, Gerald. You get out to places Brent and I can't, and I'd value whatever you have to say. Longarm, you won't mind if we jaw a little, will you?"

Not that any of the other three was likely to object to anything the senator wanted. The question had been . . . what did they call that? It took Longarm a moment to remember. Oh, right . . . rhetorical, that was it. The question was what they called rhetorical.

Longarm cleared his throat, touched his coat once to make sure the crinkling folds of paper were there where they should be, and then settled down to enjoy some fine whiskey and even finer cigars along with accomplishing a bit of official duty here at the senator's home place.

Chapter 13

Longarm sat on the side of the bed in his balbriggans, his bony knees and hairy legs dark against the white of the sheet in the dim hint of moonlight that filtered in through the French doors.

It was late and he was tired, but he wasn't yet sleepy. Part of that was because of the way his stomach knotted and groaned, reminding him that dinner had been tasty but not filling. And quite a while earlier too.

He considered sneaking downstairs to see what he could find in the pantry. But then that wouldn't be polite. More to the point, it was the sort of behavior that could get a man shot if his hosts didn't know who it was that was rambling about in the middle of the night.

With a sigh he got up, the bedsprings creaking, and fumbled on the nightstand for his cheroots and a match. He lighted the thin cigar and then, as there wasn't any ashtray in the room that he'd noticed, went out onto the balcony to smoke it.

The night air was cool and fresh and felt good filling his lungs. It came drifting in off a thousand miles of rolling, unfenced prairie, scented with grasses and wildflowers and freedom.

Somewhere out there a coyote yipped a plaintive love song, and somewhere out there cattle slept.

Longarm was glad he hadn't been able to sleep. He was enjoying being alone in the night.

A second coyote spoke to the first. Then another sound, much closer, reached Longarm's ears.

"Uh . . . uh . . . uh . . . uh . . ."

"Darling, oh, my darling, yes."

"Uh . . . uh . . . uh . . . uh . . ."

"Hard, yes, wonderful, oh, I love you so much, yes."

"Uh . . . uh . . . uh . . . uh . . ."

Longarm felt a rush of heat into his cheeks. The guest bedroom where he was—where he was supposed to be but at the moment wasn't—was next door to Miss Gayle's room. The master suite, and they'd been sure to make the point so he would know, was all the way down at the other end of the upstairs hall. The senator and Miss Gayle were staying under the same roof but *not* together.

Right.

It was sure as hell the senator's voice that rasped and moaned now, though, while Miss Gayle panted encouraging blandishments in his ear.

Bedsprings rattled, and the bed frame shook. The senator grunted and humped for all he was worth, and after a minute or so Miss Gayle stifled a thin shriek.

A few more seconds and things got quiet.

Mercifully quiet as far as Longarm was concerned.

He honestly didn't mind who fucked who. But damned if he wanted to have to listen to them do it. Not while he was alone, especially.

The thought of Senator Walker sweating and rutting atop that sleek and glossy young thing Lillith Gayle . . . it was enough to get a man damn well worked into a lather.

Longarm shivered a little, although the night air was not cold.

"Before breakfast?" he heard the senator ask.

Lillith laughed. "You're so naughty, Georgie-bear. So deliciously naughty. I love it. Before breakfast then. I'll come to your room. Make sure you're naked, darling. Do you sleep on your back? Good. Leave your door ajar so there won't be any noise when I come in. I'll slip in silent as a mouse and burrow under the covers to find you." She giggled. "Have you ever awakened with your gun in someone's mouth, Georgie-bear? Would you like to? Oh, I can hardly wait. And don't you dare wash now. I want to taste our love on you, dearest. And I want to swallow you, all of you. I want you to come in my mouth, darling, and I want to swallow you right up. Would you mind that, Georgie-bear? No? Before breakfast then. Ha, ha. Quiet now. And thank you. Thank you so much for loving me. Good night, dear."

There was a rumbling whisper that Longarm couldn't make out—just as well, probably; he was bad enough off without that too—and then, very faintly, the sound of a door closing.

Longarm shuddered again.

Of a sudden his cheroot didn't taste half so nice as it had a little bit earlier, and the breeze off the prairie felt chilling and unpleasant. He tossed the partially smoked cigar off the balcony and once again shivered.

Thinking it was something he should have done considerably sooner, he withdrew into the solitary bedroom that was his for this long, lonely night.

Chapter 14

The night might be long, he discovered, but not necessarily lonely. He'd no more than crawled back under the sheet than a shadowy figure appeared outside the French doors and he heard the muted sound of the doorknob turning.

Longarm silently reached for the Colt .44 that hung in its holster on the bedpost. He sat up again and waited.

The door swung open and a slim figure ghosted inside the darkened bedroom.

There was enough light given off by the stars and a hint of thin moonlight in the night sky to outline the shape of the intruder.

Longarm shoved the Colt back into its holster and cleared his throat loudly.

"Oh!" Miss Gayle jumped half a step back, both hands clutched to her breast.

"You're ruining the view," Longarm complained.

"What? Oh. I wouldn't have thought you could see."

"Well enough," he admitted.

"In that case . . ." She let her hands fall to waist level and stood where she was, turning just a bit to show off for him.

There was plenty enough reason for the woman to be vain about her looks. She had a figure that would have looked just fine as a Grecian statue, all swells and softnesses.

She was naked—no surprise to him—and her body was lightly sheened with sweat so that what light there was played across all her curves and hollows with devastating effect. Her moist flesh gleamed in the moonlight like warm and pulsing bronze.

Her tits stood as proud without any support as they had when she was clothed, and her waist looked even smaller. Her legs were slender and her hips nicely rounded.

All in all, Longarm would have to say, she was quite the morsel.

"Well?" she asked.

"Nice," he allowed. He reached for another cheroot and lighted it, deliberately keeping his eyes and his attention on the task of building a good coal instead of using the bright flame as a way of getting a better look at Lillith Gayle's luscious body. When he was good and ready he shook the match out, still without looking at her again, and leaned back to puff on his smoke.

"Am I disturbing you, Marshal?"

He grinned. "Ain't you really asking if you *aren't* disturbing me? I mean, you come in here t' disturb me in the first place, didn't you?"

"Don't be such a smart-ass."

"I've tried not t' be. Lots o' times. Never had much success at it though."

"Do you intend to just sit there?"

"Sit, smoke, after a bit get me some sleep. Why?"

"Damn you."

He grinned again, his face wreathed in pale smoke and his eyes reflecting the red light from the glowing tip of the cheroot.

"Are you going to make me ask for it, damn you?" Miss Gayle complained.

"Look," he said, "you're an awful fine-looking woman. You want compliments? All right. Feel free t' take all you want. You got a body a man could wallow all over. You make my dick hard an' my breathing heavy. You got tits firm enough to hang clothes on, and an ass that fair makes men wanta bark at the moon. You got all that an' good looks too. Is that what you wanted t' hear, lady?"

"It wasn't listening to mere words that I had in mind when I came here, Deputy Long."

"No?"

"Don't you want to make love to me, Deputy? Don't you want to put that hard dick inside me now?"

He shrugged and puffed on the cigar, cocked his head to one side, and squinted to keep the rising smoke out of his eyes. "No," he said thoughtfully, "I don't really think so."

The words he heard coming out of his own mouth kinda surprised him. They really rattled Lillith Gayle. "What?" she blurted out.

"I said no, I don't reckon I want t' screw you right now." He meant it too, by damn, as he discovered when he repeated the refusal. "But I thank you for the offer just the same."

"But . . . but . . ."

He hoped she didn't up and ask for an explanation. He wasn't real sure he'd be able to give her one.

It was a combination of things, he supposed. Sort of. The core of the matter, though, now that he had a moment to think on it, was that after listening to the senator romp and rut on top of this gorgeous woman . . . dammit, it really had nothing to do with the woman belonging to another man, she wasn't married or anything after all, and anyway, it wasn't Longarm's place to fret about either Lillith Gayle's morals or George Walker's horns . . . no, it was something much more basic than that, he finally decided.

The simple and unvarnished truth was that he found the idea of screwing Miss Gayle right now to be . . . unsanitary.

She hadn't had time enough to so much as wipe herself off after the senator had dismounted and left his seed sticky and matted in the hair on her snatch.

And at this particular moment, Longarm just didn't care for sloppy seconds, thank you all the same.

So he crossed his legs—his erection had mercifully subsided again—and smoked his smoke with considerably more dignity and calm than Miss Gayle was managing.

"You . . . you . . ." she sputtered.

"Sorry," he said since that was the polite thing to do. He didn't much mean it, but he did want to be as polite as possible to the senator's fiancée.

"But . . ."

"I am kinda hungry, though. Would it be all right if I was t' go downstairs an' see can I rustle up a snack?"

"You son of a bitch," she blurted out.

"No snack, huh."

"You bastard."

"Hell, I didn't think a piece o' pie would be worth all that much fuss, lady."

"You . . . you . . ." She was too pissed off by then to think of any words strong enough for the occasion. She settled for stomping her foot. Hard. Which was a mistake as she was barefoot and the hardwood flooring was much stronger than unprotected flesh. She stomped. Squealed aloud in pain and anger. Then turned and stormed back out the French doors to the balcony and the night.

Longarm sighed and drew deep on the cheroot. He sure would have enjoyed a slice of pie or something. Even another little dish of that flan custard stuff.

But he supposed it wouldn't be a real good idea to go wandering around in the dark house right now. Lordy, but that woman had been steaming when she left.

He chuckled a bit and tapped the ashes from his cigar into one of his boots—he was gonna have to remember to empty it out of there come morning, or else wash his socks again quicker than he'd intended—and decided he wasn't going to have as much trouble getting to sleep tonight as he'd thought.

Fact of the matter was—and it didn't make much sense to him, yet was undeniably so—he was feeling right good about himself now. He expected he'd be able to sleep peaceful and innocent as a babe this night.

Chapter 15

Miss Gayle did not make an appearance at the breakfast table come morning. Longarm didn't know if that was because the lady was pissed off at him or because she was so awfully worn out from serving the senator already. He didn't much care either.

As for the senator, that worthy gentleman seemed in mighty good spirits to greet the new day. Real relaxed and happy.

Perhaps because Miss Gayle couldn't make it and there was already a place set, Senator Walker sent for Carl Brent to join them. The foreman seemed a mite out of sorts, but then he probably would have rather been left alone to deal with the men than fetched over here to the big house to perform for visiting strangers. Even so, he did his best to be polite and not allow his impatience to show overmuch.

Brent ate quickly, smiled whenever anyone looked his way, and as quick as he reasonably could asked to be excused. "We have those first calf heifers being held on the flat below that old coyote den—you remember the place, the one where those pups spooked Willie Turner's horse last year and he landed upside down in all that soapweed—and I want to be there my own self. Looks like at least ten, twelve of them young she-critters will be springing today, and if I'm not there to keep those boys' minds on business they're likely to get to skylarking."

"Is that crazy Hofmann boy with them?"

"Yes, sir, and I know what you're thinking, but I'd rather you didn't ask me to fire him. I know he's a cutup and all that, but the only thing wrong with him is that he's a little high-spirited at times. There's no real harm in him. And he's the best hand I have when it comes to birthing a calf or gentling a foal. He has the gift for it."

"Whatever you think best then."

"Thank you, sir." Brent stood and reached for his hat—the wonder was that he'd taken it off even at the senator's table—and nodded to Longarm. "Nice to see you again, sir. Is there anything else I can do for you before you go?"

"Not a thing, Brent, but I thank you."

"Any time, sir."

Longarm stifled an impulse to smile. Sir, indeed. Carl Brent couldn't be more than a year or two younger than Longarm, if that. But then Brent probably had plenty of practice at being nice to the senator's distinguished guests. A deputy U.S. marshal would be mighty small potatoes around here.

The foreman touched the brim of his hat and bobbed his head, then hurried out to where he belonged.

"Seems like a good man," Longarm observed.

"He is for a fact." The senator pushed his chair back a few inches and dropped his napkin onto his empty plate. "How about a cigar, Longarm?"

"One of those like you were good enough t' share last night?"

Walker smiled. "The very same."

"In that case, sir, I couldn't hardly say no, though I really shouldn't be dawdling."

"When you're sitting here at my invitation, Longarm, you aren't dawdling at all. You're simply keeping Marshal Vail's fences mended."

73

"Yes, sir." Longarm couldn't quite decide if that not-so-subtle reminder was supposed to carry some sting in its lash or not.

Walker rang a small brass bell, and a moment later a middle-aged Mexican showed up carrying the humidor Longarm had last seen in the senator's office. The man presented first the cigars and then a silver tray containing a cutter and burning candle. Longarm gave a fair performance of the ritual, he thought, first trimming the twist off the tip of the fine, pale stogie, then warming it before he finally clamped it between his teeth and lighted it off the candle.

"Nice," he said, not having to stretch the truth even a little bit.

Senator Walker went through the same routine and then waved the Mexican away. "Yes, indeed," the politician said, sending a stream of pale smoke toward the ceiling.

"You know, Longarm," the senator said a few moments later, "I've always been especially fond of Marshal Vail."

"Is that so, sir?"

"Indeed it is. I have a certain amount of influence in Washington too, you know, not just in Denver, and I must say that I've always made it very clear just how highly I regard the marshal. Very professional fellow, he is. Very efficient and effective. As I'm sure you know even better than I."

"Yes, sir, Billy's a mighty fine fella indeed."

"Has a good future ahead of him, I'm sure," Walker said.

Longarm managed to keep from laughing. It wasn't real easy, but he managed it. Why, shee-double-it. Walker had slipped when he'd done that, making out like Billy Vail had ambitions and George Walker was just the guy to stand behind him.

What he'd gone and done by implying such a thing was make it clear that he knew Billy only as a distant political acquaintance and not as any kind of a close friend.

Why, the only ambition Billy Vail had, at least when it came to politics, was that he be allowed to do a good and honest job as United States marshal.

Billy was a peace officer, plain and simple. That was what he was and all he wanted to be. There wasn't any other job in government that he wanted. Nor, Longarm suspected, any other that he could've been talked into taking.

Good old George Walker didn't have a clue about that, though. Probably would have been incapable of understanding it if Longarm tried to tell him about it. Some men simply thought ambition had to do with *more* instead of *better,* and would have had a tough time trying to figure out the difference.

Still, the senator had been dead-sure right about one thing. Longarm's job at the moment was to keep the fences mended, not go knocking them down. So all he did in response to Walker's silliness was nod and smile and politely say, "Yes, sir."

"When you get back to Denver, Longarm, you might want to remind the good marshal that I would be deeply appreciative of his help with the Pembrooke case."

Longarm frowned.

"He's decided against helping me?" Walker asked.

"Sir? Oh. No, it isn't that at all. I was trying t' recall what this Pembrooke thing is, that's all."

"David Pembrooke is a young man who has been accused of stealing property belonging to the United States government. To wit, a draft horse assigned to the use of a, um, survey party."

"I reckon I do recollect something 'bout that. Never heard no names or details much, but I know there is such a case. Wasn't mine t' look into or I'd know more."

What Longarm didn't bother to add was that it was the same case the governor's aide Barry had been pestering Billy about just a few days ago.

It occurred to Longarm that this was one of those deals where if Billy wanted to play the game he could sure pick up some easy markers that could be called in later. Billy could get himself in good with both the governor and the senator and have the two of them owing him favors.

And if Longarm remembered rightly, this Pembrooke case was one Billy really didn't care all that much about anyhow. Real minor deal, the only question being would the defendant appear in a federal court or a state one.

It was coming back to him now, sure. The testimony and prosecution would be the same regardless. Longarm doubted it mattered to Billy much. Hell, Billy'd as good as said so. There'd been something about Billy being reluctant. Sure, now he remembered. Billy hadn't been real sure he ought to expose the young fellow to a penalty as severe as hanging, which was possible in a state court when the charge was horse theft, when the same crime in a federal court could result in no worse than a few years behind bars.

Longarm grunted and, opening his mouth before he particularly thought about what was fixing to come out, mentioned that to the senator.

"Is that what has been holding things up?" Walker asked.

"Now, Senator, I shouldn't ought to've said anything, I s'pose. I'd take it back if I could. But, well, now that I've gone an' stepped in it, I do think that's what's been bothering the marshal 'bout the idea o' turning that case over t' the state to prosecute, sir."

"Commendable of him, of course. I've always said Marshal Vail was a particularly sensitive and considerate man."

"Yes, sir."

"And of course he knows more about the young, um, defendant than I?"

"Really, sir?"

"Yes. I suspect your Marshal Vail knows this Pembrooke lad personally. As for myself, I've never met the boy. I've only heard about him. All of it good, I assure you, else I'd not involve myself in the matter."

"No, sir, I'm sure you wouldn't."

"My point being that I am certain Marshal Vail has excellent reason to be concerned about the young man's well-being and future, um, rehabilitation. And of course to insure that he does not pay the ultimate price for what was, after all, perhaps no more than a youthful prank. Believe me, I know from first-hand experience how playful these young cowboys can be. They are constantly pulling pranks on one another."

"Yes, sir."

"It would be terrible for one of these find lads to lose his life over such a thing, wouldn't it?"

"Yes, sir, I'm sure it would at that."

"I tell you what, Longarm. When you return to Denver, please tell the marshal that I can assure him the Pembrooke boy would not be subjected to so severe a penalty as that."

"You can give that kind o' assurance, Senator?" Longarm asked.

"Well, ahem, perhaps I misspoke. Just a trifle, you understand. Perhaps 'assure' is not the word I wanted. Suffice it to say that, um, it would be most improbable that any such, uh, penalty could be considered."

Longarm shrugged. "What you're saying then, sir, without actually saying it, is that you have the circuit judge in your pocket an' if Billy gives you Pembrooke the deal includes a cap on the sentence. If he's found guilty, that is, which he ain't until or unless a proper trial says so. Point is, if Billy turns him over he won't hang. Might spend time in the pokey, but he won't hang."

"That is not, ahem, precisely what I said."

"No, sir, I know it is not. That's what I think you meant. But I never once heard you *say* any such thing, and couldn't no prosecutor nowhere get me to say you actually said it, because you didn't."

Walker cleared his throat again. "Perhaps this conversation is going too far, Longarm. Let's speak of more pleasant things than crimes and hangings, shall we?"

"Yes, sir." In other words, the message was all right but the senator didn't want to get hung out at the end of a limb with it pinned onto his chest.

"Will you be going back to Denver from here?" the senator asked, striking out onto neutral ground.

"No, sir. Castle Rock. Got a few things t' look into up there." Longarm couldn't see any point in bringing up Eudora Parks and her problems. To a man like George Walker the loss of a couple of young steers would seem about as important as losing a toothpick. The senator wasn't likely to have either information about or interest in so picayune a matter as that.

"If there is anything I can help you with . . ."

"Thank you, sir, but your kindness an' hospitality here 've been more than I could've hoped for a'ready." Longarm took the offer as a bit of a hint too, and stood up to reach for his Stetson. His gear was already packed and put into the vestibule so he could collect it on his way out. "Reckon I'd best be goin' now, sir. I hope you'll give Miss Gayle my thanks an' my good-byes, sir. I surely hope she's feelin' well this morning. Sorry I missed seein' her so's I coulda told her good-bye my own self."

"I shall be sure to convey your best wishes, Longarm."

"Thank you, sir. For everything." Longarm offered his hand, and the senator gave it a limp, politician's handshake. "And I'll talk t' Billy about . . . things . . . when I get back."

"Good man, Longarm. Good man."

Longarm picked up his stuff and went out to see if he could find his horse and saddle somewhere in the maze of the Rafter W headquarters.

Chapter 16

Castle Rock was a three-hour ride from George Walker's Rafter W. Longarm figured he could have made it in two hours if he hadn't had to spend so much time zigzagging back and forth to go around all the flat-topped mesas that littered the grasslands just east of the Front Range foothills.

The mesas between Castle Rock and the Lark Ranch railroad spur were rugged things that from some angles looked like huge battlements. Or, not surprisingly, castles. For the most part they were flat as tables—hence the name *mesa*—on top and had sheer or nearly sheer sides facing west and south. From the north and east they were apt to be a little less severe, so that a man afoot or sometimes even a horse could scramble up with little difficulty. The north and east slopes were generally covered with grass and cedar, while the loose and rocky talus slopes below the sheer stone battlements on the west and south sides were more likely to show a little scrub oak or spreading juniper.

Longarm couldn't look at them without thinking in terms of watch towers and defensive positions. Why, a man with a good spyglass could see quite literally for miles from such a height. And a cannon placed atop such a natural redoubt would be virtually unassailable.

Not that such warfare had ever been conducted here in the past, nor was any likely in the future. Still, it was what Longarm invariably thought about when he passed among these ancient mesas.

Then he reached Castle Rock, a town situated at the base of one of the smaller mesas, and his thoughts returned to the business of the moment.

The sheriff's office was in the basement of a handsome granite and marble courthouse. Longarm had known the Douglas County sheriff for some time, although not particularly well.

"Sheriff Selkirk, good t' see you again, sir."

"Longarm! What brings you to this neck of the woods?"

The two men shook hands, and Longarm helped himself to a seat.

"Something exciting going on that I can help you with, Longarm?" the sheriff asked.

"Nothing real exciting," Longarm admitted. "I got a couple papers to serve in your district. If you've no objection, that is."

"You know better than that, I hope."

Longarm smiled and offered the sheriff a cheroot, then lighted one for himself. "We all know we can count on things t' be on the up an' up in this county, Milt. Leastways it'll be like that long as you have anything t' say about it. Ain't a one of us fed'ral boys ever questioned that."

Sheriff Milt Selkirk acted like he was fixing to preen and purr under that application of butter.

"Common courtesy t' let you know, o' course," Longarm rambled on. "Also, I got a question t' ask you 'bout one o' your cases that kinda overlaps one o' ours."

"And what would that be?"

Longarm told Selkirk about the loss of Eudora Parks's steers and the thin hook of federal jurisdiction in the case.

"I remember the lady coming up here, oh, several months ago that would have been, Longarm. She wanted to file a complaint."

"Yes?"

Selkirk spread his hands. "It isn't our case."

"No?"

"Out of our jurisdiction, Longarm. The lady lives down in El Paso County. That's where she needed to swear out her complaint."

"Is that so?"

"Yes, of course."

"That's what you told her?"

"I'm sure I did, I . . ." Selkirk paused, then frowned. "Or did I remember to do that? Let's see. I recall for sure her coming in here. And I remember she told me she'd lost some cattle. Then . . . let's see. I think . . . I think I might've said something about looking into it. Then I found out her property is in El Paso County, so it wouldn't be our case to investigate. But did I tell the lady that? I think I did. I mean, I must have."

Longarm grunted, but refrained from saying anything. Milt Selkirk really was a pretty good fella.

"You know, now that I think back on it what I think happened was that after the lady left I asked Jason Buddiger—do you know Jason?"

Longarm shook his head.

"Jason's one of my deputies. Nice boy. You'll like him. He comes from down in the south part of the county, so naturally he's the one I thought of when Mrs. Parks came in. Anyway, I asked Jason to look into the case. He's the one checked at the courthouse and told me it isn't our jurisdiction. I should have written Mrs. Parks a letter, shouldn't I?"

"What did you do, Milt?"

"Why, I can't exactly remember. Not for certain sure. I think I asked Jason to tell her that next time he was down

81

that way. Or maybe I only meant to." Selkirk dug a finger into his ear and drilled around in there for a while. "You know, I just purely can't remember which I did, Longarm. Must be getting old, ha, ha." The man was probably somewhere in his sixties, certainly not old enough to be getting senile. On the other hand, he was neither a gifted peace officer nor a talented administrator. Mostly Milt was a completely well-intentioned and thoroughly honest fellow. Most times that was all that was required of a county sheriff, and he had been getting elected and re-elected to office here since long before statehood.

"Do you want me to wire Jason to come back here, Longarm, so you can talk to him?"

"Wire?"

"He's down in Colorado City to testify in the Raines case. He'd been down visiting with his girlfriend that day and volunteered to be sworn in when they formed the posse. He won't be back here again till the trial is over. Unless you want me to call him back to talk to you, that is."

"No, if I need to speak with him I can always take the train down."

"Whichever you prefer." The sheriff leaned forward and dropped his voice to a whisper. "What do you hear about the Raines boys, Longarm? Will they hang?"

Longarm shrugged. It was common enough for civilians to think a deputy marshal would have an inside track on such matters. But Milt should have known better. The truth was that Longarm's guess would be no better than anyone else's. Far as he could see, no one could ever figure out in advance which way a jury might jump. Even in a case like the Raines matter.

The Raines brothers, Bell and Garland, had held up a tourist excursion coach the previous spring. The coach had been carrying a party of visitors from New York on a day-long picnic and sightseeing trip through the red sandstone formations known as the Garden of the Gods. The robbery had been straightforward enough, and would have caused no great excitement except that the older of the brothers, Gar Raines, had become smitten with a young lady in the group and announced his intention to make her his bride. The girl, little past her twentieth birthday, had been forced to accompany the robbers when they fled the scene. The posse had not rescued her until two days later, and rumor since had been that unspeakable acts had been performed upon her while she was the captive of Bell and Gar Raines.

Longarm's opinion was that there was more imagination than truth in those rumors. Nevertheless, the kidnaping and chase and now the trial had all been as sensational as the newspapers could make them.

The Raines brothers had been as good as convicted from the first moment of their capture. The only real question was whether they would hang or be granted the mercy of life imprisonment.

"Well?" the sheriff asked. "Have you heard anything or not?"

"Haven't heard no more than you, Sheriff," Longarm confessed. And then, seeing how disappointed Selkirk looked, he added, "But if I was t' guess I'd say them boys will hang. That's what folks seem t' want, so I won't be surprised t' see it happen."

Selkirk grinned. "That's exactly what I was thinking too, Longarm."

"What'd you say this Jason fella's name was again, Sheriff?"

"Buddiger. His papa worked for me when I was first in office, back when this was still a territory. Buddy, we called him. Damned if I can remember his right name. Good man he was, though. Got thrown from a horse one morning and landed wrong. Busted his neck. He was paralyzed and laid in bed like a lump for six, eight months until he finally passed over. That was when Jason was just a button. Jason's mama remarried later. I never forgot the boy, though. Was glad to take him on when he came looking for a job last fall. I haven't had reason to regret it since neither."

"I'll look him up if I need to, Sheriff. Thanks."

"Anything I can do, Longarm. You know that."

"Yes, sir, thank you."

"Did you want me to go with you to serve those papers you said you have?"

Recalling the "help" Vance Hollowell gave him down in Palmer Lake, and the results of that help, Longarm respectfully declined the Douglas County sheriff's offer.

"If you change your mind . . ."

"Yes, sir, I'll be sure an' ask if I do."

"Or if you want Jason back here. It's only a little more than an hour away by train, you know, and the truth is that Jason could be up here working and still be on call for when the lawyers want him in that courtroom. The reason I haven't been doing it that way is for one thing Jason isn't much when it comes to paperwork; he's at his best in the field. For another, this way he gets to spend some time with that girlfriend of his while El Paso County pays his travel and day wages. It lets my budget stretch that much further and keeps Jason happy too." Selkirk chuckled and winked.

Longarm laughed a little too and stood, his knee joints popping. "Good to see you again, sir. Thanks for all your help. I'll be sure an' tell Marshal Vail how nice you've been."

Selkirk beamed. "Why, thank you, Longarm. And don't you forget now . . ."

"Yes, sir, I know. Any way you can help."

"That's right, son. Any way at all."

Longarm made his way out into the midday heat, his stomach grumbling in a none-too-subtle reminder that breakfast had been a good many miles back.

Poor Mrs. Parks, he was thinking. Two different deputies had been asked to look into her losses, and the both of them had believed she lived outside their jurisdiction. Silly. But such things surely happened. It was up to him to correct their errors now.

He looked around for the nearest cafe but then, remembering the last time he'd been to Castle Rock, made a beeline for the Polly Wolly Doodle. There was a girl waiting tables there who . . .

Chapter 17

The rest of the day proved to be nicely productive. And the promise of the evening wasn't bad either.

During the afternoon Longarm was able to serve three subpoenas without so much as anyone scowling at him.

And that night Celeste Carracker was eager to see him as quick as she was off work.

Just how good could things get anyhow?

On Celeste's advice, Longarm took a room on the second floor of the boardinghouse where Celeste stayed. Overnight male guests were welcome in the parlor and at meals, but they were allowed to go no higher than the second floor, where their rooms were located. The female boarders, who stayed on a more or less permanent basis, had rooms on the third floor and in the dormer above it.

There was only one stairwell leading to the third floor, and a door on the landing leading up to it was barred and locked promptly at half past nine each evening. The proprietress of the establishment, a prim and priggish spinster who was chairwoman of the local Temperance Society and who nipped constantly at bottles of Dr. Brinkman's Herbal Bitters, personally oversaw the lock-up operation and stood watch over the staircase like a gargoyle lurking over a cathedral's chilly eaves.

Celeste assured Longarm, though, that Mrs. Pendergast was not quite so all-seeing, all-knowing, and all-hearing as she believed herself to be.

Consequently Longarm had an early supper at the Polly Wolly Doodle—the better to find a few free moments in which to whisper promises back and forth—and then faced a stretch of some hours before Celeste could be collected from work and returned to the monastic isolation of the boardinghouse.

A small libation seemed in order. And perhaps a friendly turn of cards.

"You son of a bitch!"

The voice rang out shrill and excited in the smoky, brightly lighted room.

Men in all directions froze in place while they tried to assess the intent—and more important the location—of the unhappy fellow who was making the noise.

"You cheating bastard."

"Liar, I never."

"Cheater."

"Liar."

"Oh, shit." The last voice was Longarm's. The men who were doing the shouting were at the table adjacent to his.

His own game was low stakes and friendly. Obviously that was not a statement that had universal application throughout the room.

There were, however, some generalities that could reasonably be applied among the patrons of the establishment.

Almost to a man, for instance, they were now silent, the exceptions being those inebriated gentlemen who were screeching at one another.

And almost to a man the good fellows of Castle Rock who happened to be present were busy placing their cards, drinks, whatever, gently onto the tables before them.

"You bottom-dealt me, you son of a bitch."

"You blind butthead, I don't hafta cheat to beat the likes of you."

"Cheat."

"Liar."

"Nobody calls me that an' gets away with it."

"I will, damn you. Liar, liar, liar."

They sounded to Longarm like a pair of eight-year-olds.

On the other hand, not too many eight-year-olds carried guns. These two sure did.

"Fill your hand, you son of a bitch."

"You first, cocksucker."

There was a sound not unlike the roll of thunder or perhaps the approach of a stampeding herd of buffalo. Men were vacating their chairs and moving swiftly to the sides of the room. No one, however, seemed interested in leaving. It was only prudent to get out of the direct line of fire. But no one wanted to miss the sight of whatever bloodshed might transpire here.

Longarm, common sense somewhat modified by the dictates of duty, stood and tried to inject a note of reason into the situation.

"Hold up there, dammit," he barked.

The sound of his voice might as well have been a starter's whistle.

As soon as Longarm spoke, both angry combatants grabbed for their weapons.

It occurred to Longarm that he was standing directly behind one of the duelists and that this was not a particularly wise thing to do.

While the gentlemen were fumbling for their guns Longarm

beat a hasty retreat in the same direction all the others had taken seconds before.

The first fellow, a man in sleeve garters and a derby hat, dragged his revolver out and aimed it point-blank across the table at his opponent. In his excitement, however, Sleeve Garters forgot to cock the revolver. He frantically jerked on the trigger over and over again, his face red with fury that the damn gun wouldn't fire.

Meanwhile the other man, a balding fellow wearing a suit and ascot, was having difficulty getting his revolver out of his pocket. The hammer spur had become somehow ensnared in a tuft of loose threads, and he could not pull the gun free.

"Damn you."

"Liar."

"Cheat."

Sleeve Garters ineffectively squeezed his trigger again and, frustration boiling over, ran around the table to deliver a kick on the left thigh of his opponent.

"That isn't fair," Baldy shouted.

The combatants having moved about now, there was a fresh field of fire around them, and the spectators, Longarm included, did a quick side-shuffle to correct things.

Baldy gave the butt of his gun a mighty heave, ripping the gun free amid a tangle of cloth and lining material and leaving the pocket of his coat flapping at his side like a bird's broken wing.

Baldy shoved the little break-top revolver forward, squeezed his eyes nearly shut, and began shooting.

Sleeve Garters turned pale and doubled over, vomiting down the front of his trousers, the hot fluid streaming across his forearms and hands—and gun—as he braced his arms on his knees.

Baldy, meanwhile, had spent his ammunition, all five shots flying somewhere in the general direction of the ceiling.

The saloon quickly filled with the competing stinks of gunpowder burnt in too close quarters and fresh puke. Neither of those was a smell that Longarm found particularly attractive. On the other hand, either could be considered more welcome than the bright copper scent of fresh blood.

Sleeve Garters was still retching, and Baldy was shaking now and drenched with his own sweat.

Sleeve Garters hadn't ever actually fired a shot. Baldy hadn't hit anyone.

Longarm figured the whole thing could be counted a draw.

"Somebody better go get fetch a constable," Longarm suggested.

"Why?" someone else asked him.

"All right," the bartender was saying, "which of you is gonna clean up this mess?"

"I will," Sleeve Garters said in a small, weak voice. "Just give me a minute, will you?"

"I'll help," Baldy offered.

"You will?"

"Yeah. But, Jesus."

Sleeve Garters rolled his eyes heavenward. "Yeah. Ain't that the truth."

"Jesus," Baldy repeated.

The smell of gunpowder was receding. The other was not.

"If you fellas don't mind," Longarm said to one of the gentlemen he'd been playing with, "I think I'll cash in."

"Say, you aren't letting that little ol' thing chase you off, are you?"

"No, I just got to meet somebody in a few minutes."

"All right then. Maybe you'll join us again tomorrow."

"Maybe," Longarm said. He touched the brim of his hat. "G'night, gents."

"G'night, Long."

He went out into the clean, clear night air with some relief, and paused on the plank sidewalk to fill his lungs, then began a slow stroll in the general direction of the Polly Wolly Doodle.

It was still a little early to pick up Celeste, so he ambled back and forth through the quiet, sleepy streets of Castle Rock, in no hurry at all and at peace with the world.

As for it being at peace with him . . . well, that wasn't for him to decide.

Chapter 18

"Good night, Miss Carracker."

"Good night, Mr. Long."

"Sleep well."

"Thank you, you too."

"Yes, well, ahem, good night then."

They shook hands briefly and Celeste went up the stairs under the watchful inspection of Mrs. Pendergast. The door at the landing closed with a solid thump. Longarm tugged the watch from his vest pocket and grunted. Eight more minutes and the door would be barred and locked until morning. He turned and ambled off in the direction of his room.

"Evenin', Marshal."

"Good evening." He couldn't remember the name of the fellow boarder who greeted him in the hall.

"Care for a nip before you turn in? There's a nice place just around the corner and I'm headed that way myself. Be glad for the company if you care to come along."

"That's mighty nice o' you, but I'm 'bout used up for one day. Think I'd best turn in now. I tell you what, though. If I'm still in town tomorrow night maybe we can get together for the evenin'."

"That'd be fine," the friendly fellow said with a smile. "Good night then."

"Good night."

Longarm entered his room and carefully bolted the door shut behind him. He left the table lamp unlighted and made no immediate effort to go to bed. The extent of his undressing was merely to remove his hat, coat, and vest so that he was in shirtsleeves and trousers and still had his boots on. He took a seat in the lone chair in the room and smoked a cheroot without haste. Then, judging that enough time had lapsed, he went to the window of his room. And climbed out.

A narrow balcony, more decorative than functional, circled the front and both sides of the boardinghouse. Longarm followed it to the north end of the building and turned left. At the back of the house the balcony ended, but it was only a long step to the roof over the kitchen lean-to. And that took him to a sturdy trellis that had never known the presence of the ivy it was intended to carry but which showed the wear and tear from a great many boot and shoe soles over the years.

Longarm stood on the rooftop and whistled softly between his teeth. Immediately a window above was pushed open.

"Custis?" a voice whispered.

"Yep."

"Come up. Hurry."

Longarm scampered up the ladderlike trellis—somebody had been thinking when he built the thing because it was at least five times heavier and more secure than any trellis ever needed to be—and went in through the window where countless nocturnal callers had gone before.

Celeste took a moment to give him a kiss of greeting—the greeting included grinding her pelvis and soft belly against him—and then led him by the hand through the darkened hallway.

"You'll have to keep your voice down, dear," she explained

93

once they were safely behind the latched door of her room. "Mrs. Pendergast is only two doors down. She can't hear half as well as she thinks she can, but there's no sense in finding out just how much she *can* hear. You know?"

"I'll try an' be good."

"Honey, I've been with you before, remember. You aren't just good, you're terrific." She gave him a bawdy wink and giggled a little.

"You, uh, don't have a roommate, do you?" he asked, nervously glancing in the direction of a second bed in the tiny room. The thought of company coming in in the middle of things was a trifle unsettling.

"I do but she's sleeping with Jenny Cornwall tonight."

"You didn't tell her—"

"Of course. Don't look at me like that, Custis. I didn't tell her *who,* for gosh sakes. I just told her I needed the room to myself. I do the same for her, after all. More often than she has to move out for me. Not that she's a slut or anything. She just . . . why are we discussing this?"

"Damn if I know," Longarm admitted. He took Celeste into his arms and shut her up with a kiss long and deep enough to make her knees sag.

"Wow," she murmured into his mouth, then began exploring in there with her tongue.

"Mm hmmph."

"Mhhmph mm."

He began unbuttoning her dress while she returned the favor with his buttons.

By the time they broke off the kiss they were both half undressed and breathing hard.

Celeste grinned and whirled away from him in a sudden pirouette, her skirts flaring and the front of her dress falling open to expose her breasts.

Celeste Carracker wasn't the prettiest girl Longarm had ever been with, but she wasn't a beast either. She had a full—all right, over-full—figure with melon-sized tits that were pasty and pale and crisscrossed with blue veins showing just under the skin. She had a slightly thick waist and powerful legs. She also had appetites that were what a fella might call lusty. Celeste Carracker was no shy, shrinking violet.

She preened and pranced a little before him, showing off while she stripped the layers of cloth away until she stood there naked and beckoning. She lay down on the narrow bed and spread her legs wide apart so he could see the moist, pink thing that was peeking out from its nest of curly brown hair.

"Now ain't that pretty," he whispered.

Celeste giggled and reached down to touch herself and spread the lips open. Light from the bedside lamp caught the moisture that coated her flesh there and made it gleam and sparkle.

Longarm shucked out of the rest of his clothes and stood over her.

Celeste gasped and sat up so she could reach him. "I'd forgotten how big and nice you are, Custis." She touched the side of his cock with the fingers of one hand and giggled again when it bounced and jumped. She poked lightly at the taut-stretched head and was rewarded with another lively response. "Oh, my."

"Havin' fun?" Longarm asked dryly.

"As a matter of fact, yes, I am. Now hush a minute and let me play."

She experimented to see what would, or what would not, make it jump and jiggle like that. It turned out that nearly any contact, whether with hand, lip, or tongue, would achieve the desired end.

Each of those several methods delighted Celeste and spurred her on to new experiments.

The flutter of an eyelash certainly worked. So did a puff of hot breath.

She finally failed with the too-slight brush of a wisp of hair.

"Darn," she complained. Then she shrugged and abandoned that particular form of play. She lay back flat on the bed with her legs spread wide apart. "Do me now, Custis. Please."

"Oh, I dunno." She'd had her play. Now it was his turn.

"Custis! Please."

"Sure. In a minute."

He sat on the edge of the bed and leaned down to kiss her. She didn't mind that.

He cupped his hands over her breasts and squeezed, lightly at first and then harder. Celeste's breath quickened and became harsh and labored as she began to squirm and wriggle. He rubbed his thumbs over her thick, rubbery nipples. He continued to knead her left tit in one hand while with the other he roved across her belly and into the wet, overheated orifice of her pussy.

"Custis. Please." Her hips pumped and gyrated as she tried to force his touch deeper.

"In a minute, I told you." He pulled away from her there and massaged her belly for a moment while he slid his hand back up her body to take hold of her tit again. He squeezed with both hands, very hard this time, and Celeste's hips lifted off the bed in eager response.

"Do you want to spank me, Custis? Do you want to hit on me? I'll let you, Custis. If that's what you want."

It wasn't. But quite frankly it pleased him to know that she would let him do that to her if he wished.

Instead he let go of her tits, leaving white marks where his fingers had been, marks that quickly darkened and turned red after he released his hold on her.

He rolled over her and poised for a moment between her

thighs while the inquisitive head of his cock nuzzled at the wet womanflesh of her.

Then, finding the smooth entry, he plunged forward without warning, thrusting deep inside her.

Celeste cried out. Her head thrashed back and forth on the pillow, and she wrapped herself tight around him, clinging to him with arms and legs alike so that he could not have pulled away from her if he'd tried.

Not that he had any intention of leaving.

He plunged and battered, assaulting her belly with the hard planes of his masculinity and filling her body with his massive tool. The harder he pumped the more frantically Celeste thrust herself up to meet him.

He built quickly, too quickly, but he was beyond wanting to contain this first wild coupling. He went at her like an animal, tearing into her flesh as if to conquer what had already been given as a gift.

Fortunately Celeste did not mind the violence. She returned his pounding thrust for thrust and gasped for more.

Within moments, much too soon, Longarm stiffened, the sides of his neck corded with straining muscle and tendons. A groan ripped out of his throat as he exploded inside Celeste's body, pumping hot fluids into her in a seemingly endless spasm of raw pleasure.

He held himself rigid like that for several moments.

And then he collapsed onto her warm, sweat-slick body.

He was so thoroughly spent that he was trembling.

Celeste hugged him gently and crooned into his ear. "Oh, darlin', honey, sweetheart, how awful nice that was, how awful nice."

She held him with arms and legs alike and rocked him slowly to and fro, taking virtually all of his weight onto herself and holding him still inside her.

"How sweet an' dear a man you are," she whispered.

He nuzzled the side of her face and kissed her, and when he did he could taste salt. He pulled back a fraction of an inch and looked at her, and saw that she was crying.

"Damn, I went an' hurt you, didn't I?"

"Oh, no, honey, you never hurt me, you never. These is tears of joy, sweet Custis, because I don't reckon I ever been with any man that needed me more'n you did tonight or that showed me so much down deep caring. But you didn't hurt me, sweetheart. Can't no man ever hurt no woman like that. Not when he's lovin' on her, he can't."

"If you say so," he conceded.

"Oh, I do, honey. I promise you never hurt me. You gave to me, more'n you likely know." She kissed him, the kiss this time tender and gentle, and he wiped the tears off her cheek with the ball of his thumb.

"You didn't get anything outa it this time, though. We'll have t' do something about that next time around."

"Custis honey, I got everything a girl could want outa that just now." She giggled and winked. "But I won't say no if you wanta do the things that make my toes curl and my eyes go all blurry and red. I won't mind some of that too. But the real important stuff, honey, you already gave me plenty of. Don't you never think different."

He kissed her and sighed.

"Here now," Celeste said. "Get off me, honey. I know what you need to bring that sweet thing of yours back up. No, don't you be trying to do anything. You just lay back . . . that's right, on your back, just like that . . . you just lay there with your eyes closed and see can you figure out what it is that's doing things to you . . . no, don't you peek, that'd be cheating now, wouldn't it."

He could hear her giggle softly.

Could feel things too now.

Soft things. Warm. Slow and subtle. Here. There. Some so

faint he wasn't entirely sure he was feeling them at all.

But Celeste was right about one thing for sure.

She damn well knew how to arouse his interest once again.

Longarm kept his eyes tight shut and smiled and smiled and smiled.

Chapter 19

Longarm tugged the other boot on and stood, careful not to stamp his feet to settle into the boots because he didn't want to make the noise. He reached for his gunbelt.

"Do you have to wear that even here, honey?"

He smiled. "No, o' course not, but I'd rather wear the thing than try an' carry it when I'm climbin' down that trellis again."

"I suppose that makes sense," Celeste conceded.

Old habit made Longarm buckle the belt in place just exactly the same as always, with the buckle centered on his stomach and the butt of the big Colt immediately to the left of the belt buckle, the black holster canted at precisely the best angle for a speedy cross-draw. Not that he actually expected to have to draw down on Celeste. He smiled and opened his mouth to say something to that effect to her.

He was interrupted by a loud explosion that shattered the peace of the night. There was the explosion and the sound of broken glass falling.

"What was—"

"Shotgun. Now hush." Longarm started for the door. The shot had sounded awful close.

The first shotgun blast was followed by the sound of another, this one seeming even closer and this time with no broken-glass noises afterward.

"Dammit, that's inside this house, I b'lieve."

"Custis . . ."

"It wasn't no farther away than the other side o' this here house, Celeste." He reached the door in two long strides and opened it.

"No . . . wait, Custis. Let me check the hall. All right, there isn't anyone . . . no, not that way, the landing door's locked, remember? You have to go down the trellis."

Longarm frowned but changed direction.

At least two bedroom doors along the hallway were opened, but quickly shut again when the occupants saw there was a man on the floor. Longarm hoped all the girls who lived there were as accommodating and understanding with each other as Celeste and her roommate, but he didn't want to take the time to fret about that now.

He hurried back through the room and down the trellis, not even thinking to tell Celeste good-bye, and stepped from the kitchen roof over to the narrow balcony.

No one was in view on this side of the house, so he quickly moved forward, pausing at the corner before he showed himself above the street.

There was no one on the ground that he could see, but there was a dark, shadowy figure on the balcony at the far side of the place.

He saw the shape dimly and only for an instant. Then it disappeared toward the back of the house on that side.

Whoever it was that'd fired those shots . . .

No, better to reach no conclusions before he had himself some facts.

Even so he palmed his Colt and eased carefully along the balcony until he came to the broken window that had to be where the shots were . . . shit!

101

It was his room that had the window broken out.

He looked inside. There was no sound and nothing moved, but the sharp, acrid smell of burnt gunpowder hung strong in the air. Damn!

He hurried the length of the balcony and peered around the corner, but there was no shotgun-wielding gunman to be seen there now.

Whoever it was that had fired those shots was gone. If indeed that had been him that Longarm had glimpsed moments earlier.

There was no sign of anyone on the balcony or on the ground either. Longarm stood there only for a moment, acutely aware that he would make a fine target if someone—say, someone with a shotgun—was hiding in the shadows below. Then he withdrew and climbed back into his room through the empty window frame.

"Mr. Long? Are you all right in there, Mr. Long?" It was Mrs. Pendergast's voice. She was banging on the door he'd bolted shut hours earlier.

"I think so, yes." He went to the door, his boots crunching over splintered shards of glass, and drew the bolt.

His landlady, lamp in one hand and a ring of keys in the other, stood in the hallway in her nightclothes. She looked small and frail and very frightened, her fear translating itself into bluster.

"What happened, Mr. Long? Have you been shooting guns off in your room?"

"No, ma'am, I haven't. An' I don't rightly know yet what did happen."

The woman sniffed. "You are all right and you say you've not been shooting guns, but I want you to know, sir, I will stand for no more noise. Not in my house."

"No, ma'am."

"Oh, dear. You've broken the window. Look there. Don't

you try and deny it, young man. I can see for myself."

"Yes, ma'am."

The landlady pushed indignantly inside the room, and by the light of her lamp Longarm got his first look at the damage.

Pretty damned interesting damage it was too, he would have to say.

He touched a broomstraw to the flame of Mrs. Pendergast's lamp so he could light his own bedside lamp and turn the wick up for a better look.

The window was broken, of course. He'd already known that. And one curtain panel had been shredded by the shot.

More to the point, though, was the fact that Mrs. Pendergast's bedding had been peppered with shot too.

Whoever it was who'd fired those shots had been aiming them through the window square at the bed inside.

The bed where Deputy U.S. Marshal Custis Long should have been asleep and unaware.

Now wasn't that just downright interesting.

Somebody'd come wandering by in the middle of the damn night and taken a notion to blow away a federal officer. Yeah, that was real interesting, he thought.

Two shots. From a scattergun. The method was generally right efficient.

If it hadn't been for Celeste . . .

"I have no idea what you have been up to in here, sir, nor do I wish to know. But you will pay for the damages. Indeed you will. And I will thank you to find other accommodation for tomorrow night, if you please."

"Yes, ma'am," Longarm said. He didn't really feel like having a spat with Mrs. Pendergast at this hour.

He didn't feel much like crawling into that bed to sleep either. Just because the night-walking fellow with the shotgun had left once, that didn't necessarily mean he couldn't come back and try again.

If he knew he'd missed, that is. Could well be that he'd triggered off his rounds and lit a shuck without ever realizing the bed he'd dusted was empty of the intended victim.

Still and all, there wasn't any sense in counting on that.

Longarm bobbed his head and agreed to all the landlady's peevish complaints, then bolted the door closed behind her as quick as he decently could.

Once alone he pulled the mattress off the bed, and dragged it into a corner beside the wardrobe so he could maybe get a little sleep tonight after all.

And this time he didn't undress before getting into bed. He took a pillow and blanket and lay down fully dressed and with the Colt .44 beside his ear.

If anybody wanted to try for seconds tonight they might not find the repeat version so easy as the first had been.

Fortunately—or not so fortunately—there was no further disturbance during what was left of the night.

Chapter 20

Milt Selkirk rolled the tiny balls round and round on the top of his desk, using the tip of his forefinger to run them this way and then that while he stared thoughtfully into the far distance.

"One thing," he said at length, "it wasn't any professional assassin that shot at you last night."

"No," Longarm agreed, "it wasn't." He paused and added, "Or if it was he's the cleverest I've ever come across."

Selkirk grunted and looked down at the lead pellets Longarm had dug—over Mrs. Pendergast's protests—out of the mattress, pillows, and bedroom wall this morning. "What would you say, Longarm? Number one or two?"

"Thereabouts," Longarm said. "Way smaller than buckshot, that's for sure."

"So what you're looking for," the Douglas County sheriff surmised, "is somebody that usually hunts goose but last night decided to bag himself a marshal instead." The sheriff, Longarm noted, might be more politician than policeman but he wasn't stupid either.

"Looks just about that way," Longarm said. A grown, healthy man shot even at close range with goose shot would have probably a fifty-fifty toss-up chance of survival. Buckshot, being considerably larger and heavier and therefore able to penetrate much deeper into the body, would have had a far greater likelihood of delivering a lethal wound. A killer with any degree of skill and experience would know that. The average cowboy or homesteader might not.

Sheriff Selkirk rolled the pellets around on his desk some more while he pondered the situation. "Know what I think?"

"What's that, Milt?"

"I think you're making your cow thief awfully nervous somehow. I mean, it's pretty serious stuff to go shooting at a federal marshal. Most generally you boys get your backs up about that sort of thing."

"Yes, sir, you could say that."

"You must be close to your man then, mustn't you?"

Longarm grinned. "Milt, I've been thinking that exact same thing half o' last night and all o' this morning. Truth is, if I'm close t' knowing anything about whoever it is that's stealing old Mrs. Parks's steers, then I sure as hell don't know it my own self. I might've stumbled all over it, but I sure ain't seen it. Not t' recognize, I haven't."

"I wish I knew something to tell you. Maybe if Jason was here . . ."

"Maybe," Longarm said doubtfully.

"You say you've talked to Vance Hollowell and to me."

"That's right. And I've brought it up, just kinda in passing, to a few other folks too. None of them acted like they had anything t' hide when I spoke with them. I'd near about swear they didn't."

"Strange," Selkirk said.

"Yes, sir, it surely is."

"I wish I knew what to tell you, Longarm. I can promise you one thing. If I hear of anything or just think of some new angle that we haven't already considered, I'll be sure and let you know. Quick as I can. It's always possible, you know, that your boy with the goose gun will try again once he learns he's missed you."

"Don't I know it. Until I figure this thing out I'll have to ride loose."

"I don't envy you," Selkirk said.

Longarm shrugged. Milt Selkirk might well have never had anyone intent on killing him. That was a claim Custis Long hadn't been able to make for many and many a year now, going all the way back to the war years, when there were entirely too many fellas on either side of that business wanting to shoot down everybody wearing a different color pair of pants.

Still, it wasn't the sort of thing a body really got used to.

Or wanted to.

"Where do you think you'll go from here?" Selkirk asked.

"I have one more subpoena to serve. I reckon I'll handle it, then go back down to Mrs. Parks's place and see if she can tell me anything more that'd be helpful. If that doesn't work, I dunno, I might look up this Jason of yours and see if he can think of anything. You said he knows that end o' the county pretty good, I believe."

"Knows it about as well as it can be known, I'd say, him growing up down there and everything. Mind now, if you want me to pull him back here I'll be glad to do it."

"No, you leave him there where he is. The way things work you can be sure the day I'd want t' talk to him up here is sure as hell the day them lawyers would be yammering for him down there too. Better if I just plan on goin' down t' him if I need."

"All right then."

"If you need t' reach me you can send wires out addressed t' catch me at Palmer Lake, Monument, or Colorado City. Leave word all them places an' I'll bump into at least one o' your messages."

"And if there is anything I can do . . ."

107

"I appreciate it, Milt. I surely do."

Longarm stood and shook hands with the sheriff, then went back over to the boardinghouse. He was not especially popular there this morning, but he had to go head to head with prune-faced Mrs. Pendergast one more time, else she'd be filing complaints with the Justice Department and creating problems for Billy Vail just as sure as God made pissants. What Longarm was wondering now was whether he could slip those damage charges past Henry on the lodging voucher or if this one was gonna have to come out of his own pocket. He figured he would at least try to get the government to stand good for that expense. Hell, they could afford it better than he could anyhow.

Chapter 21

It took Longarm most of the day to find the man named on that final subpoena. Not that the fellow was trying to avoid him nor that the place was so far away. It was just that people kept giving him contradictory directions about how to get there.

He eventually found it northwest of Castle Rock, a small outfit set astraddle a dry creek bed in the foothills. The place was called Robson's Roost, which at this low elevation didn't make much sense until Longarm saw what manner of livestock Paul Robson raised there. Turned out he was a chicken rancher and proud of it.

"Let me show you around, Marshal. No, I insist." Robson seemed a real nice fella, and Longarm would no doubt have liked him a whole lot if he hadn't smelled so much like the chickens he raised.

"See how I got them all in runs there? They can't go nowheres but inside to the roosts and nest boxes or here in their own little runs. One lot can't mix in with another either. I can keep them sorted any way I need."

"How come you put that net over the runs?" Longarm asked. It seemed a waste of time and money to contain a bunch of birds that can't fly anyway.

"Hawks, Marshal. Lots of hawks around here. I used to lose

an awful lot of birds to hawks and eagles and owls and such. Now they can't get down to where my babies are."

Longarm grunted. Like anything else, he realized, there is a logic to each and every business even if an outsider might not recognize it on first inspection.

"Good business chickens. I recommend it. Yes, sir, a man with chickens never goes hungry, ha, ha. You got eggs to sell, pullets to raise to lay still more eggs, cockerels to butcher and sell for meat. There's always a market for fresh meat, you know. Especially around these parts. And with chickens, why, even their shit is valuable. I got vegetable farmers that come to me from thirty, forty miles off. Had one fellow come on the train all the way from Florence just on the off chance I'd have some extra to sell him. You wouldn't believe what a truck farmer will pay for a load of aged chicken shit either."

"I'm sure I wouldn't," Longarm mumbled.

"If you ever give up on marshaling you could do a lot worse than go into the business of raising chickens, let me tell you. Good money in it."

"I'm sure that's so."

"Think about it. And if you want to take it on, you come right back here to me. I'll tell you all you need to know. Help you get started. Everything."

"That's real kind o' you."

"You, uh, wouldn't mind putting in a good word on my behalf with the U.S. Attorney up there in Denver, would you?"

"I'll tell him you accepted service without a fuss if you like. If I see him before your date t' show up, that is." There wasn't much likelihood of that, but Longarm saw no reason to make an issue of it.

"But that's what I mean, Marshal. I can't take time away from my babies to go all the way up there to Denver. Surely you can see that. Why, what would they do without me to take care of them?"

110

"Same thing they do when you're away selling your eggs or fryers or whatever, I reckon."

"But that's different, Marshal."

"Is it for a fact?"

"Yes indeed it most certainly is. That is genuinely necessary business. Not like . . . you know."

Longarm shrugged. "You do whatever you think best, Mr. Robson."

"Does that mean I don't have to go?"

"No, sir, it means you oughta do whatever you think is right. Means you can show up on the day it says on the paper there an' tell them lawyers whatever they want to know. Or else you stay down here an' tend to your chickens. If you do that the court will issue a warrant an' then me or one o' the other boys will come back down here an' arrest you an' carry you up t' Denver for a few days. Either way you'll have your time in court t' say whatever it is you're gonna say. But you got your choice how you want t' get there." Longarm was smiling gently. "Like I say, Mr. Robson, you do whatever you think is best. That's what a man surely ought t' do every time."

"I, um, see."

Longarm touched the brim of his hat. "Good day t' you, Mr. Robson."

"You son of a bitch."

"Does that mean you won't help me set up a chicken ranch after all, Mr. Robson?"

"Bastard."

"Not that I know of, sir, but I'll look into it. Bye now." Longarm returned to his horse and mounted. He rode away from the chicken-shit place and headed south.

It was late by then. The closest place he knew of where he would for sure be welcome overnight was down at John Lark's ranch. But that was too far to make it in before ten or eleven at night. And anyway, with John at home, either he would end up frustrated as hell because he couldn't sneak into Cathy Sue's bed, or else he would find an opportunity to lift her skirts, in which case he'd end up feeling guilty as hell. He wasn't in a humor for either frustration or guilt at the moment, so he figured he'd best bed down out there on the grass where he was rather than ride late.

The country there at the base of the foothills was actually flatter than it was over east where the big mesas were. Except in the creek beds where some soil had accumulated, it was mostly red gravel and clay that supported a little grass suitable for light grazing. Where conditions were right for it there were wide swatches of scrub oak that attracted both the lowland whitetail and high country mule deer. There was a little cedar and a few runty spruce, but otherwise not much in the way of trees.

Mostly there was grass and sky and the jagged, ragged wall of the mountains to the west. Longarm found it to be country that a man could breathe deep in.

The sun was long past disappearing behind the mountains, and the foothills and nearby plains were held in the long shadow that extended twilight here for hours. Longarm found a likely-looking creek with a trickle of sweet water in the middle, and followed it up until it was no more than a handspan wide and running between sloping, grassy banks.

He dismounted and hobbled the red horse, then turned it loose downstream from the sheltered spot where he intended to make his bed. There was clean water and good graze and no reason in the world for the animal to wander. Which probably meant that by morning it would be just as far away from there as the hobbles would permit. But then that was just part of the deal when a man depended on something as notional and contrary as a damn horse for his transportation.

He smoothed the tall, lush grass down and laid his blanket over that for a mattress. Clumps and clusters of dead scrub oak trash provided fuel for the small fire he would need to make his coffee. The cheese and biscuits and jerky in his saddlebags needed no cooking. And a small fire was best anyway. The best idea of all was to finish with the fire before it got full dark so there would be no light to draw attention to him up here at the head of this shallow draw overlooking the plains.

He got the fire built and the coffee water to heating, then walked up to the top of the sharp ridge overlooking his campsite and took a long look around.

He could see the railroad tracks in the distance to the east. Except for that, though, there was no hint that mankind had yet found this particular corner of the earth.

Longarm liked that thought. He stood tall and breathed deep of cool, clean air that was untainted with the stink of smoke or garbage.

He stayed there until he heard the hissing, spitting splash of water boiling over onto his coals. Then he ran down to snatch the lid off the coffeepot, only burning his fingers a little bit when he did so, and dumped a handful of the ready-ground coffee beans in. He pulled the pot away from the fire and poured in a little water cold from the creek—to settle the steeping grounds—before he put the lid back on. In a couple of minutes the coffee would be ready and then he would eat.

In the meantime he pulled out a cheroot and lighted it with a twig dragged back from the fire.

Sometimes, he thought, life was pretty damn good.

Chapter 22

Longarm came awake. Immediately and fully. This was no slow wakening from a peaceful rest. It was sudden and heart-pounding, and he had no idea why.

Something . . .

There was a crackling in the dry litter that surrounded the scrub oaks. Something heavy and very much alive was moving there. Several somethings. Deer, he quickly realized. Browsing deer that have no reason to be quiet are noisy as hell.

But that was not what had brought him awake. He was certain of that. The sounds of grazing horses or moving deer would not disturb him no matter how loud they got.

This must have been something quiet and subtle. Something like . . .

He grimaced and pulled the Colt from the holster so carefully placed beside his head.

Something like the slow, sneaky steps of a man trying to creep silently up the creek bed. Almost silently, that is. He wasn't bad at it, but he wasn't near good enough at it either. Longarm could make out each individual footfall now.

He guessed the distance at forty, maybe fifty yards down the draw.

The fellow—was it likely he held a shotgun in his sweating hands? yeah, Longarm thought maybe he did—was moving extra slow and careful now. One foot at a time. That meant he was scared. He was having to maintain his balance on each foot in turn while he crept forward that least little bit each time. A man who knows what he's doing spends most of his time with his weight taken on both feet at once. He moves soft but he's careful not to be stupid about it. This fellow was scared, all right, and not very well versed at the game he was trying to play here. Longarm could sense that easily in the way the would-be assassin moved through the night.

Scared, yes. But determined. He kept coming on, after all.

Just like he'd kept at it last night in Castle Rock. He was determined as all hell, for he'd shattered the quiet of the sleeping town with that first shotgun blast but stayed long enough to fire the second and try to make sure of his kill. Hell, even with goose shot he might have accomplished it if Longarm'd been in bed where he belonged.

So, yeah, this guy might be an amateur and he might be scared, but he was sure as hell willing to gut it out and come ahead.

It was a quality that Longarm failed to find admirable under these particular circumstances, never mind what he might otherwise have thought of such gritty determination.

Longarm slipped out of his bed and moved with ghostly silence into the shadows beneath a nearby spruce. The moon had set for the night but the sky overhead was clear, and there was starlight enough that the gunman should be able to make out the dark shape of the bed. The light was poor enough that he shouldn't be able to tell that it was empty. Not unless he got closer than Longarm intended to allow.

What Longarm figured to do was give the fellow time enough to hang himself. So to speak.

Let him come in just as close as he wanted. Let him drag his hammers back and take aim.

Then challenge him.

Real loud.

A fella as nervous and scared as this one seemed to be would likely shit his drawers at the sound of someone bellowing at him outa the night.

With any kind of luck he'd jerk the triggers of the scattergun and empty his weapon into thin air. Then it would be child's play to wrap him up and take a look at him.

Longarm still couldn't see why anyone would want to kill over something as inconsequential as a few lousy head of dairy cattle. But Longarm was certainly willing to allow this gent to educate him on the subject. Preferably from the inside of a jail cell.

Longarm hunkered down in the shadows of the spruce tree and waited.

He could see a dark, shadowy lump in motion now. Forty yards, give or take a few. Thirty-five. Thirty. The approach was taking forever. Longarm was willing to wait that long if that's what it took.

Suddenly, dammit, there was another shadow. Longarm tensed for a moment, then relaxed. The second figure was large and boxy in shape. Too big for a deer. And too close to the approaching human anyway. So it was Longarm's horse. The grass was so good there that it hadn't wandered far from where he'd turned it loose. It had been standing on the upstream side of a scrub oak thicket.

Now, probably because the presence of humans often meant grain, it stepped out to meet the gunman. Who wasn't being half as sneaky as he thought he was.

The gunman took a step forward. And the horse stepped out from behind the brush toward him.

It must've been a helluva sight, Longarm conceded, a big

116

old thing coming unexpected out of the night like that.

But, shit, the guy didn't have to react like that, did he?

He screamed.

"Jesus, Mary, an' Joseph!"

And he threw up his hands to ward off whatever demon this was.

He happened to be holding the shotgun in those same hands.

And he was scared.

And whether by accident or by intent, his panicky, clenching fingers yanked back on the triggers of the gun.

There was the scream.

Then a huge ball of yellow fire spreading at the base of twin spears of more fire.

The horse reared.

The man whirled, fell down, bounced up as quick as a ball of India rubber thrown onto a hard floor, and began running like all the hounds of Hell were nipping at his heels.

And probably, Longarm thought, the guy thought they were.

"Shit," Longarm said aloud.

Which pretty well covered the subject.

Whoever the persistent gunman was, Longarm wasn't going to make his acquaintance this night.

Hell, the way he'd torn out after the red horse had startled him, Longarm probably couldn't catch the fellow now if he had the red horse and a relay of five more just like him.

That guy probably wouldn't stop running till sometime past noon tomorrow, Longarm guessed.

Longarm bent down and shoved the Colt into its holster.

Then, frowning, he straightened as another sound reached him from down the creek a little distance.

"Shit," he said again.

And with a heavy heart, already knowing what he would

find, he started down the graveled creek bed toward the horse he could hear thrashing in its death throes on the ground.

That panicked blast from the twin muzzles of the assassin's shotgun had found a target after all.

Well, he'd more or less wanted the guy to empty his gun when he jumped, hadn't he? But not this.

Damn it to hell anyway.

Chapter 23

By the time Longarm humped his gear all the way down to John Lark's place he was cranky as a toothache bear coming out of hibernation.

His feet hurt, his belly ached, his left arm had a cramp in it . . . and worst of all he had to look John in the eye and tell the man he'd gone and allowed a good horse to get killed.

All in all he would have to say that he'd had better days than this one.

"Custis." Cathy Sue came flying out the back door with a towel in one hand and ripping a grease-spotted apron over her head with the other. "Where did you come from? And where's Red Boy?"

Longarm scowled and shook his head.

Cathy Sue skidded to a stop just short of throwing herself all over him. Which meant her papa was somewhere near, else she'd have been climbing him like a squirrel goes up a pecan tree. For the same reason too. To get to the nuts. This time, though, she stopped a foot or so from him and occupied her hands with wringing the apron and towel together in one big knot.

"I'm sorry, Cathy Sue. Some sonuvabitch went an' shot him."

"Oh, Custis! Are you all right?"

"Yeah, I'm fine, but I owe your daddy a mighty good horse."

"You're sure you're all right?"

"Fine. Really."

"Are you hungry?"

"I could eat, that's for sure. Wouldn't mind settin' down for a minute too."

"Come inside." She raised her voice. "Netty? Papa? Custis is out here and he's hurt. Papa, you come help him, won't you? And Netty, put something on the table. He hasn't et in two days." Apparently excitement was gilding the lily here. More than just a little bit.

"Dang it, Cathy Sue, I already told you I'm fine. And I ate this morning before I broke camp. I just didn't want t' carry everything so I left the rest o' my supplies behind. So quit makin' stuff up, please."

"Why, Custis Long, you're wore purely to a frazzle even if you won't own up to it. I love you and I can tell. Now you hush and do what I say."

John Lark came outside in a rush, a napkin still tucked under his collar, so apparently he'd been having a late dinner himself. "Are you . . . hell, Custis, I don't see you dripping blood anyplace. How bad off are you?"

"I'm fine, John, which I already told your daughter three times. I'm all right except for bein' ashamed o' myself."

Lark frowned.

"It's about your horse," Longarm said, then briefly explained.

"Better Red Boy should take those shells than you, Custis."

"Thanks, John, but I feel bad about it. That was a nice horse. I'll pay you for him, o' course. Whatever you think he was worth." Longarm had already concluded that if John's price was above the government allowance for saddle mounts, Longarm would make up the difference himself and not quibble for a change.

"Oh, hell, I don't know. We'll talk about that later. You look a mite dusty, Custis. Dry too. Come inside and we'll fill you up and, um, find something to wet your whistle too. Don't you be looking at me like that, Cathy Sue. If I can't offer a drink to an old friend, then what's the point of living?"

"Daddy," she warned. "You promised me . . ."

"I was hung over when I said all that. Anything a man says when he's hung over don't count."

The girl sighed and marched off toward the house, snapping orders at the long-suffering Netty before she ever reached the back steps.

"Come along, Custis," Lark said. "And don't you worry about anything as minor as a dead horse, you hear? I'm just glad you're all right. You say this jehu was creeping up on you and . . . how was that again? Why, you could have been ambushed anyplace between there and here. Weren't you worried about that?"

"Aw, a fella with a shotgun isn't gonna worry me much in broad daylight. Time he could get close enough to do me any hurt he'd be too close for me t' miss spotting him. It's only at night or in a crowd that I'd have t' fret about this guy,'specially since he ain't real good at it."

"It sounds worrisome enough for me, Custis. But then I've never been shot at. Haven't ever shot at anyone else either, I'm glad to be able to say. I have to admit it's rather intriguing, though. Tell me about it. Every detail if you please."

"Oh, you don't wanta hear—"

"Yes, I do. I insist. I want to hear everything."

"If you say so." The two men continued inside to where the kitchen table was being freshly loaded with leftovers from the family's recent meal and with half a dozen other things that

Cathy Sue dragged out. Whatever else happened Longarm wasn't going to leave here hungry.

"I can't take this mare, Cathy Sue. This is your own horse, and don't try an' tell me otherwise."

"I don't care, Custis. I know you'll take good care of her."

"Like I done with Red Boy?"

"Papa told you you shouldn't ought to worry about that. So quit worrying at it. I swear, Custis, you're like an old dog with a new bone. Pick, pick, pick. You already gave Daddy that paper to send in to the government. That will take care of everything."

Longarm sighed. These were wonderful folks. But frustrating at times. The both of them. Cathy Sue came by her closed-ear bull-forward way of doing things real naturally.

He stepped inside the stall with the pretty little roan mare Cathy Sue called Willow. The horse snorted once, then came forward with a stiff-legged tentative gait to stretch her neck out and flare her nostrils. Horses are as bad as dogs for wanting to examine things by smell, so Longarm stood still and gave her time to sniff him over. She came closer and whuffled and snorted him up and down until she was satisfied. Then she tossed her head once, and after that was willing to stand quiet while he put bridle, blanket, and saddle on her. He left his cinches loose as he wasn't intending to ride off right at that particular instant.

"Do you have a minute, Custis?"

"For you, Cathy Sue? O' course."

"Can you keep a secret?"

"Good as most, I'd say. Maybe better."

"Promise you won't tell *any*body?"

"Ayuh, I promise."

"All right then. Follow me."

"Where?" Then he saw. The girl pulled her skirts aside so she wouldn't trip on them and scampered up the ladder into the hayloft.

"Quiet now. I don't want anyone else to find out about this."

"Then you best quit hollering your own self." He looked around to make sure they weren't being observed—Netty and John were still inside, Netty cleaning up in the kitchen and John working on his account books—and followed Cathy Sue up the ladder and into the loft. "Where are you?"

"Over here, Custis." She was whispering.

"Where's that?" he whispered back.

"To your right, then straight back. Behind the new hay. Mind you don't trip over that pitchfork Benny left laying where it oughtn't to be."

He went around behind the mound of bright-smelling hay.

And found Cathy Sue.

Damn her.

The girl was standing there in the middle of the hayloft naked as a boiled egg.

A ray of sunshine came down through a gap in the roof, picking out motes of dust in the air and making them look like tiny fireflies dancing in midair. That same small beam of sunshine played over Cathy Sue's pert and pretty body like it was some kind of magic light, pointing out all the creamy softness and gentle curves and pink, lovely hollows.

Damn her.

Longarm felt himself grow hard in spite of everything.

"I love you, Custis," she whispered.

"I know you do, honey."

"All I ask is a few minutes."

"Dammit, Cathy Sue, your daddy isn't fifty yards away from this spot. He could walk out here any second t' see what we're up to."

"He won't," she said.

"But he could."

"Love me, Custis. Just a little bit. Please."

"You know I—"

"Not in any big way, Custis. Not forever and ever and like that. I won't ask that of you. But just for right now. Hold me. Kiss me. Let me feel you inside me again. Please."

"I . . ."

"Please." She was coming forward even as she whispered to him. Coming forward. Lifting her arms. Opening herself to him. Giving of herself completely. Her body, her soul, her everything.

It would have been cruel of him to reject her.

Wouldn't it?

He found himself kissing her. She tasted of mint and berries.

Her body was tiny. And cool to the touch. He lifted her into his arms—she was so slight she seemed to weigh nothing—and carried her to a bed of soft, sweet-smelling hay. He eased her gently down and lay beside her.

"I love you, Custis."

"Thank you, Cathy Sue."

She wriggled and squirmed with pleasure, turning in his arms, arching her back, rubbing herself over him while she fumbled to free the buttons at his fly.

He started to remove his coat, but Cathy Sue shook her head. "Wait. Please. Ever since the last time you were here . . . I've been daydreaming, imagining how it would be this time. Leave your clothes on. Just open your trousers . . . like that, yes. Oh, it's so nice an' big, Custis. So hard. I do like it so." She caressed his shaft with gentle, loving care.

"Now cover me. No, don't take the gun off. I want you to leave it right where it is. It won't hurt me, really. I want to feel you the way I most always see you, with all your clothes

124

and everything. That way every time I see you but can't have you I'll have this memory to call into mind and it will almost be like you're making love to me again, even when you're standing there fully dressed. Even when we're at the same party and all the way across a big room I can look at you then and feel you inside me, feel the buttons hard against my chest and the leather of your holster cool on my stomach. Like that. Yes. Oh, yes, darlin', like that. Oh, Custis. Yes. Hard now. Don't hold back. You aren't hurting me, you'd never hurt me, I know you wouldn't, oh . . . !"

Under Cathy Sue's prompting he really did forget to hold back, and pumped into her hard and swift and deep as ever, unmindful of the sharp objects that might be poking into her soft flesh. She didn't mind and he no longer thought about it either. He dug the toes of his boots into the hay for leverage and thrust deep.

Cathy Sue whimpered and moaned and clutched him ever closer to her as her hips moved to meet him and her breathing quickened, quickened, burst over the edge. She shuddered and bucked violently beneath him in those frantic spasms that can only come from completion. She trembled and quivered, and he felt the lips of her pussy clamp hard and wet around his pulsing shaft as he reached his own climax only seconds behind hers.

He shuddered and stiffened for a moment, then sighed and would have pulled away from her.

"Wait," she whispered. "Stay. Just for a moment."

He nodded, and she pulled him down on top of her, wanting to take his weight onto herself.

After a bit she shuddered again and sighed. "Thank you, dear Custis."

He smiled and kissed the side of her neck. "Can I get off now?"

"If you have to."

"Reckon I should."

He drew back, his limp cock falling out of her with a wet plop, and crabbed backward, trying to be careful to not dribble any leftover fluids onto his britches.

Cathy Sue giggled when she saw his predicament. She took a handful of the soft hay and used it to wipe him, then impishly leaned down and took him into her mouth to finish cleaning him. When she pulled away she said, "That's to make you think about the next time."

"I got to admit, that should do the job, ma'am," he said with a grin.

"Good. See that it does."

Longarm stood and buttoned his trousers. He did half a squat to settle everything back the way it belonged, and began brushing the hay off his knees and elbows.

"Hey up there."

Longarm froze. It was John's voice. The man was standing at the foot of the hayloft ladder. Longarm hadn't heard him come in.

And here Longarm was with John's naked daughter kneeling in front of him with his seed fresh and wet all inside her.

"Hello?" John called.

"Yeah," Longarm answered, his cheeks of a sudden burning.

"What are you doing up there, Custis?"

"I'm tryin' t' seduce your little girl, John, what else would a man be doin' in a hayloft with a girl pretty as Cathy Sue?"

"Ha, ha."

"I was showing him the baby swallows in the nest here, Daddy. I told you about them but you wouldn't come look at them with me like Custis did. Remember?"

"Well come down, both of you, before I start to think Custis was the one telling me the truth."

"Yes, Papa."

126

"Be right down, John." Longarm gave Cathy Sue an exasperated look—she was pulling her dress over her head and at the same time was standing on one foot with the toes of the other foot searching about in the hay for a missing shoe—and he went on down the ladder to ground level.

"I'll be down in a second, Daddy. There's something up here I want to look at. I won't be a minute."

"Okay, honey."

Longarm, his heart pounding much worse than after a gunfight, brought Cathy Sue's little mare out of the stall and followed John outside into the afternoon sunlight.

Shee-it, he was thinking. Shee-double-it.

"Are you sure you won't stay the night?" John Lark was saying.

"Uh, no, John, I reckon I'd best be on my way. Thanks for the offer, though. And for the loan o' this horse."

"Thank Cathy Sue for that. Willow is hers to lend, not mine. Bring her back whenever you like. You know you're always welcome at this house, just to visit or for anything else you might want. Always."

Mighty accommodating folks here at the Lark Ranch, Longarm thought. Salt o' the earth, all right. He glanced back toward the barn, to where Cathy Sue was just coming out looking about fourteen years old and fresh and virginal as could be. Longarm looked back at her daddy and winced. Not that there was any taking it back. And not that he likely would've if he'd had the power to, which thank goodness he didn't.

He sighed once and determined to put John and Cathy Sue both firmly out of mind. At least for the time being.

Chapter 24

El Paso County Deputy Vance Hollowell wasn't in his office when Longarm dropped in to see him. Instead there was a note on the door saying the deputy had gone to lunch and would be back some time past noon.

"Damn," Longarm muttered.

"Got a problem, do you?" a man asked from the open doorway of the barbershop next door.

"Pardon?"

"I asked if you got a problem, friend. I mean, like if you need to see Vance in a big hurry."

"Just an annoyance, not an emergency," Longarm admitted.

"How about a haircut then?" the barber suggested.

"I just got me one last week."

"A shave then? Little bit of bay rum to make the ladies take notice?"

"You're some hand as a salesman, ain't you."

"If I was all that good at it I wouldn't have to spend so much time looking for more work, would I?" the friendly fellow said with a grin.

"You have a point there, I reckon."

128

The barber stepped out into the late morning sunshine and pushed a hand forward. "Jake Hoffman," he said, "barber, leech, dental surgeon, sometime salesman . . . and all-around good fellow."

Longarm smiled back at him and introduced himself.

"Long. Long? Say now, Vance has mentioned you. Let's see. From Denver, right? Of course. You're that Ewe Ess marshal called Longarm. Sure, Vance has spoken of you."

"I confess," Longarm said.

"Say then, Vance wouldn't mind you dropping in when he's at lunch. I'm sure he wouldn't. I mean, I wouldn't tell it to just any Tom, Dick, or Norman off the street, but Vance takes his lunch most every day over at Clara Poole's cafe. It's just a block and a half from here. Why don't I tell you how to get there. You just go down to the corner there and turn left. Then . . ."

Poole's Cafe was tiny but popular, the sort of hidden-away spot the locals kept to themselves while the tourists were directed to flashier and more expensive establishments.

Longarm was greeted by looks of mild suspicion from the working men who crowded the place, until Vance Hollowell wiped those away by standing and waving for Longarm to join him at a table in the back corner.

"Sit down, Longarm. Maybelle, bring a plate for my friend here and put it on my bill."

"Naw, I couldn't let you do that, Vance."

"Me? Hell, I'm not buying; the county is."

"In that case, I accept."

Hollowell nodded. "Will the day's special be all right or do you want a menu?"

"The special's fine, thanks."

"You heard the man, Maybelle."

"You want a beer with that or coffee?"

"A beer'd be nice."

"I'll be right back then, gents." The waitress hurried away. Longarm pondered whether he would have time for a smoke before the food came, but decided he probably wouldn't.

"Are you doing any good toward finding your cow thieves?" Hollowell asked.

Longarm grinned at him. "Lots. I just don't happen t' know what that good is, though." He explained the puzzling situation regarding the amateurish gunman.

"Odd, isn't it," Hollowell agreed.

"It damn sure is, Vance. I can't figure it."

"You haven't discussed the case with all that many people, eh?"

"You, Milt Selkirk up in Castle Rock, Mrs. Parks herself of course. Not much beyond that."

"I can't see any reason for anybody to be gunning for you then," Hollowell said. "I know I don't know or quite frankly care all that much about so minor a case, and I'm sure Milt is in pretty much that same boat."

"I wasn't suggesting . . ."

"Oh, I know you weren't, Longarm, but it's only right and natural that you'd have to think about it. It's only logical. Besides, even if I didn't have anything direct to do with it, you'd have to wonder did I mention the case to anybody else who might have some cause to get nervous. That's what I'm trying to do now is call back to mind anybody I could have talked about your case with." He shook his head. "I can't think of anybody."

"You didn't mention it to Jake Hoffman or, like, somebody setting there waiting for a haircut overheard?"

Hollowell shook his head again. "No, I'm pretty sure I never spoke of it to anybody. Had no reason to, actually. It isn't like it's an important case or anything."

Longarm sighed.

"I'll keep trying. Maybe I'll remember something. But I doubt it."

"Sure is strange," Longarm said.

Maybelle came back with the lunch special, which proved to be a cut above the normal cheap and filling sort of thing one would expect to find in such a place. No wonder Poole's was crowded.

"Is there anything I can help with?" Hollowell offered.

"Not that I know of," Longarm admitted.

"If you think of anything . . ."

"Yeah."

Longarm finished his meal quickly and declined an offer of pie to follow. "But a refill on this beer'd be nice."

The waitress brought another mug of beer for Longarm and more coffee for the local deputy, who seemed in no great hurry to rush back to the paperwork that would surely be waiting for him in the office.

Longarm buried his mustache in the foamy white suds of his beer. Hollowell stood and motioned toward someone at the doorway.

A boy with a canvas sack slung over his chest came darting past the tables. "Latest thing, Mr. Vance."

"An extra, Willie?"

"No, sir. Just the usual early edition."

Hollowell winked at the boy and handed him a nickel. Apparently this was a regular thing because the paperboy didn't even offer to make change; he just pocketed the deputy's coin and scampered away in search of another customer.

"That can't be this evening's paper, can it?" Longarm asked, noticing the masthead on the front page identifying Hollowell's reading matter as a Denver newspaper. An afternoon newspaper at that.

"Sure. Early edition, like the boy said. I don't know when they start printing, but they always make the 12:10 at Monument. Then the noon coach brings a couple bundles over here. There's always a lot of Denver folks in town, and they like their hometown papers."

"How 'bout that," Longarm marveled.

"Say now," Hollowell said with an accompanying whistle as he glanced over the headlines.

"What's that?" Longarm asked, reaching into his coat for a pair of cheroots, one for himself and the other for Vance.

"There was a murder last night. Inside the jail. Can you believe that?"

"Unfortunately I can," Longarm said. "Not all the fellas that live in a place like that are real nice folks. If you know what I mean."

Hollowell grunted and continued reading. "The inmate was one of yours too."

"Mine?"

"Not yours personally. Or maybe he was. Fella name of David Pembrooke. Do you know him?"

Longarm frowned. "Know of him but I never met him. Waiting trial on a charge o' stealing government property, right?"

"The newspaper says horse theft."

"Government horse. Kinda the same sort o' charge as this picayune little case with Miz Parks."

"There couldn't be some connection between the two, could there?"

"Naw," Longarm said. "No chance o' that. Pembrooke was in the pokey waiting disposition long before those steers was stole."

"No need to think about disposition now," Hollowell said. "Somebody took care of that the quick and permanent way."

"Stabbed, I suppose," Longarm suggested.

Hollowell took a moment to skim down through the article.

132

"Mm hmm. Here it is. A sharp piece of bedspring shoved into the ear canal. The paper says the weapon was left in place in the man's head. If there hadn't been some blood seepage from the wound they might never have noticed it."

Longarm grimaced. That statement, he reflected, said more about the quality of employee they had at the jail than about the efficiency of whoever it was that killed young Pembrooke. "One thing," he said.

"What's that?"

"Now they can stop the political bickering about who gets t' try the poor sonuvabitch."

Hollowell shrugged and grunted, then brightened and pointed to something else on the same page. "Look here now."

"What's that, Vance?"

"The Cheyenne Blue Stockings have agreed to play a series of exhibition matches against the teams in the Denver Sport League starting next month. They're speculating now that Denver will have a fully professional baseball team by next spring at the latest. How about that?"

Longarm didn't answer. His thoughts were focused on murder, politics, and cow theft. In roughly that order, at least for the moment.

And overriding all of that remained the question: Who the hell wanted to kill him? And why?

Chapter 25

After leaving Vance Hollowell—without learning anything further—Longarm forked the horse Cathy Sue called Willow and jogged the few miles to Monument.

It occurred to him that there was something he needed to check on, something that couldn't be learned in either Palmer Lake or Monument.

He put Cathy Sue's horse up at a nicely maintained livery where a boy in his teens assured him the mare would be treated like a household pet, then presented his credentials at the Denver & Rio Grande depot on Front Street.

"Yes, sir, the next southbound will be in . . ." The agent turned to squint at a wall clock. "Twenty-four minutes. Exactly."

"Exactly, eh?"

"Yes, sir. On the dot. You can wait right over there if you like, sir."

Longarm thanked the man and carried his gear to the bench indicated. He was taking his things with him even though he did not intend to stay overnight. It was just that a fellow never knew.

The D&RG southbound steamed to a clattering, brake-heating stop—it was a helluva job bringing all that weight to a halt after the speed that was generated on the downslope of Monument Hill—within forty-five seconds of the announced time. Longarm was impressed.

He waited while a crowd of laughing and happy holiday travelers disembarked from the coaches, then made his way on board.

A few minutes more and the train jolted forward, snapping and shuddering as the engine pulled through the loose couplings and was able finally to draw smoothly and powerfully forward.

Three-quarters of an hour later Longarm stepped off the train to the platform at Colorado Springs. From past experience he knew he had a walk of only a few blocks to his destination, but he would have to hurry if he wanted to catch them before they closed for the day.

Chapter 26

Longarm emerged from the stately courthouse and paused on the steps, his hands rummaging from pocket to pocket. First a cheroot—damn-fool records clerk had something against smoking and made everybody around him suffer because of it—then the Ingersoll watch.

The flavor of the cheroot pleased him. The time shown on his watch did not. Public offices and a good many businesses were already closing. He could see practically no movement in the downtown area just a few blocks up normally busy Tejon. It was getting late. Still, he would do what he could.

He walked back down to the railroad depot and got a wire off to Milt Selkirk in Castle Rock, then another to Billy Vail informing the boss about where he could be found if need be.

Longarm thought about trying to find Milt's deputy Jason Buddiger. Probably no point in even looking for him until morning, though. Buddiger was supposed to be over in Colorado City, which was only a half hour or so away by coach, but by now the city court would already be shut for the day. Longarm wouldn't know where to look for Buddiger except there. Or was that right?

He frowned. Milt had said the deputy was attending a trial in Colorado City, hadn't he? Or had he meant Colorado Springs? It didn't make much sense that a trial as notorious as the Raines case could be taking place in a city court. Why, it more likely would have been held at the county courthouse. Which Longarm had left just minutes earlier. Hell, he could have stood side by side with Deputy Buddiger up there and not known it. Mumbling under his breath a little, he went back inside the railroad station to amend the telegram he was sending to Milt.

When he came outside this time he had a distinct impression that he was being watched.

Tension pulled at the muscle across his shoulders, and the back of his neck prickled. He clenched his hands into fists and then carefully, deliberately relaxed them again so as to loosen taut muscle and prepare himself for a fight.

But there was no one to fight.

The station platform was nearly empty. An elderly couple strolled along among the benches. A cowboy with a sweat-stained hat pulled low over his eyes was napping while he waited for a train. An enterprising boy with a basket of fruit and some flyblown sandwiches waited for the customers the next train should bring.

But there was no one in sight who presented any obvious threat.

Obvious, Longarm thought. That was the thing. Just because something wasn't obvious, it didn't mean that something wasn't so.

And he could damn sure feel that some SOB was watching him.

Who? Where? He didn't know.

But he suspected he could guess.

His guy with the shotgun hadn't been around for a spell. Apparently the jehu had caught up with him again.

Longarm feigned a yawn and idly scratched his belly, placing the fingers of his gun hand conveniently near the butt of the .44 Colt.

But who was the ambusher? The kid with the fruit basket? The sleeping cowboy? Dammit anyway.

Longarm whirled and, keeping an eye over his shoulder, made his way back up the hill toward Cascade and a boarding-house that he knew and liked from staying there several times in the past.

Longarm woke in a mood that was less than perfect. His eyes felt like someone had packed them with grit while he was asleep, and they burned from there having been too, too little of that sleep to start with. He'd only dozed off and on through the night, and that had been while he sat in a cane-bottom chair. He hadn't trusted the bed, both because some smart-ass with a shotgun might want to perforate it and because the comfort that the mattress offered might have enticed him into a dangerously deep slumber. Better to groan come morning but be alive to do so.

Groan he did, though. His butt ached, the inside of his mouth tasted like fermented sheep shit, there was a painful crick in his neck, and his left foot and half that leg were still sound asleep, never mind that the rest of him had woken up.

Good morning, he told himself sourly.

He stood up gingerly, not trusting the left leg just yet, and winced as the pins-and-needles sensation tingled down deep inside where it couldn't be scratched.

Hobbling like a broken-legged duck, he made his way across the room and poured water into the washbasin. He splashed some across his face and upper body and felt a little better.

A cold-water shave really woke him up. That and the accompanying nicks and small cuts that came with it.

He could have gotten hot water downstairs, but his leg still burned and prickled some and he didn't want to go down and right back up again. Or he could have simply waited and gotten a shave at the barbershop he'd used when he was here before.

This morning he simply did not want to trap himself in the relative confinement of a barber chair with all the drapes and towels that would mean.

It occurred to him that this gunman, amateur or not, had him uncommonly spooked.

Perhaps because the guy *was* an amateur? Probably, Longarm conceded.

The thing was, with a professional, either a hired assassin or a generally talented felon, you could pretty much know how he would act under a given set of circumstances. A man could figure out when to duck and when to stick his head up and look around.

With an amateur, though, nobody knew what the fuck was gonna happen next. Not even the amateur murderer himself.

Let one of that kind get excited and he might well walk into a convention of peace officers and start shooting. You just never knew.

Fact of the matter was, Longarm was more nervous about one civilian with a shotgun than he would have been about two professional sharpshooters with buffalo guns.

Especially in town where there were so many places for a fellow to hide. Including in plain sight.

In town was where he needed to be, though, so in town was where he'd have to stay. At least for the moment.

When he was shaved and dressed he carefully packed his gear and went downstairs to the dining room of the boardinghouse.

"Good morning, Mr. Long. You slept well, I hope?"

"Fine, thanks." Wasn't no point in going into all that. Besides, if he went and complained that there might've been somebody gunning for him in the night, it seemed real unlikely that he'd be welcomed back here the next time duty brought him down this way.

"It looks as if you will not be staying longer?"

Longarm shrugged. "No way t' tell yet. Sorry."

"It is of no importance. Come back if you can. I will hold your room until last. But only until the other rooms are full, yes?"

"Sounds fair t' me," Longarm said, dragging a chair back from the table and helping himself to a nearby platter of ham and eggs.

Your room. Now why did that entirely ordinary phrase strike a note of interest in him? It shouldn't. But it did. He took some fried potatoes and some biscuits and strawberry jam. The jam was especially good. Sweet but slightly tart too and . . .

Your room.

Of course.

Last night he'd had the same room he always took here. The couple that ran the place knew him and accommodated his wishes about that. And there were three, maybe four full-time boarders who might've recalled what room Deputy Marshal Custis Long favored when he stayed here.

Yet the prick with the shotgun hadn't come calling in the night.

Longarm was positive as positive could be that the guy'd been there yesterday afternoon, looking and waiting and almost certainly wanting another crack at him.

Yet there hadn't been any attempt made last night.

There hadn't been any balcony convenient outside the bedroom window either, of course. But there had been a hallway. Longarm had spent just about the whole damn night listening to the sounds that were made in that hallway.

A gunman who knew which room Longarm was in could find out how the bed was situated inside that room if he really wanted. He could have made a try with both barrels through the wall. That would have been just about his style too, judging from what Longarm'd seen of him so far.

But he hadn't done it.

Could be something in that, Longarm realized.

Like for instance the guy'd been able to come up with exactly that sort of information at Mrs. Pendergast's up in Castle Rock, but had drawn a blank here in Colorado Springs.

Was it logical to conclude then that this idjit with the scattergun was from Castle Rock? Or at least was plenty familiar with it but didn't know beans about the El Paso County seat?

Something on that order, Longarm decided.

Not that that told him anything. Exactly. But it could provide a place to start from.

"Is something wrong with the meal, Mr. Long?"

He blinked. "Pardon?"

"I asked—"

"Oh, no, I heard you. I was just . . . wool-gatherin'. Sorry."

"So long as there is nothing wrong with the food."

"No, it's fine. Really." He smiled and proved the point by loading up his fork with a molehill-sized mountain of eggs and stuffing it into his mouth. The eggs were cold and congealed and he damn near gagged getting it all down.

But he managed it. And never quit smiling the whole time.

Chapter 27

The sense that he was being watched was noticeably absent when he walked from the boardinghouse to the railroad station, but was back in full force when he came out of the telegraph office.

Dammit, anyway. As before, he couldn't begin to figure out which of the people on the platform was his gunner. If any of them was, that is. The guy could be anywhere within a quarter mile watching through a spyglass . . . or might be the fellow standing at Longarm's elbow, the one who *looked* like a traveling salesman. That could be a perfectly innocent sample case sitting on the platform boards beside the man's feet. Or the bag could hold the taken-down pieces of a sawed-off shotgun. It was big enough, if barely.

Dammit, Longarm thought, he was starting to imagine things now.

He took another look around—today the platform was crowded, as people came to greet new arrivals from the south or else to board the next train north—and told himself to quit being such a damned old woman.

He settled for taking a cheroot out and lighting it, then passed the time by admiring the ladies in the crowd. There were five positioned where he could get a good look at them and three of those worth looking at more than once. Not a bad percentage, really.

He puffed on his smoke and tried to visualize how each of the three woman would look without their garments intruding on things.

But in the back of his mind he couldn't quite put aside the strong, strong sense that someone not far away was watching him still. And waiting.

It was with no small sense of relief that Longarm finally joined the others who were pushing forward to board a north-bound D&RG coach.

Next stop, Monument.

Chapter 28

Longarm rode loose in the saddle of Cathy Sue's little mare, but that was a matter of long habit and not immediate necessity. The feeling that he was being watched had stayed with him to Monument and on to the livery stable—whoever this fellow was, he was a tenderfoot when it came to killing but he could damn well stay out of sight whilst following somebody—but had stopped right there. Longarm would almost be willing to swear that he hadn't been trailed back to Mrs. Parks's place.

Normally that might be expected to worry him. After all, it isn't enough just to keep someone from bushwhacking you. It also helps if you nail the sonuvabitch to the wall to make sure he won't be trying it again.

This time, though, Longarm figured he would quick enough learn who it was who'd been behind him all this time.

A couple of minutes with Mrs. Parks should clear all that up for him, he figured. At least in light of what he'd learned yesterday at the El Paso County courthouse, and now this morning in the telegram from Milt Selkirk.

He drew rein in front of Mrs. Parks's house, and dismounted without waiting for an invitation. He tied the mare to a post and let out a whistle to announce himself.

"Over here, Mr. Long. I'm in the milk shed."

"Yes, ma'am." He had to **duck low to avoid** bumping his head on the thick timber lintel. The milk shed was half dugout, half sod house. The thick walls and dim interior kept the place cool inside regardless of what the temperature might be outdoors. It was perfect for storing milk. Longarm found Mrs. Parks busy pouring milk through muslin strainers, dumping it from the buckets she used when she collected it into steel cans for transportation to town. "Can I help?"

"If you like."

"Yes'm." There wasn't any way he could stand and watch while this scrawny little old woman muscled buckets and milk cans around. The cans in particular were damned heavy once they were filled. Longarm set his coat and Stetson aside and rolled his sleeves up a couple laps. "You pour, I'll carry," he said.

"Thank you." He held a folded length of clean muslin over the mouth of a can while Mrs. Parks poured raw milk through it. The smell of the milk was warm and heavy and tickled the insides of his nostrils. The homey chore reminded him of when he'd been a kid. "I hope it is good news that brings you back, Mr. Long," the old woman prompted.

"Uh, not exactly, ma'am."

"No? What then?"

He hesitated.

"Bad news?" she asked.

"Not exactly, ma'am. I just . . . ain't real sure how t' bring this up."

"I believe you will find with most things, Mr. Long, that the best way is to be blunt. Please do be. At my age I no longer appreciate surprises, and I certainly have no admiration for coyness either."

"Yes, ma'am. The thing is, ma'am . . . are you sure you want me t' . . ."

145

"Out with it, Mr. Long. Please."

"Yes, ma'am. Well, the thing is . . . Miz Parks, you been cheating on your taxes. That's it, isn't it? Why your property ain't listed on the tax rolls in either county?"

The old lady stopped pouring and set the bucket aside. She looked even older when she fumbled her way to a seat on one of the milk cans that was already filled and closed. "I was afraid that would come out," she said.

"How'd it happen, ma'am?"

"By accident, really. This was, oh, several years back. Along about the time they were getting ready to change from territorial government to statehood, I think, although I don't know if that had any bearing on anything. Be that as it may, a nice young man from El Paso County came out to talk to me. I gave him a cup of tea and thanked him for his interest and told him my property was in Douglas County. Which it is. Some of it. I wasn't being entirely untruthful."

Longarm cleared his throat but didn't say anything. Hell, what *could* he say?

"A week or so later another nice young man came by. He was from Douglas County. He didn't want any tea, but he did like the fresh bread I'd baked that morning. We had a nice talk, and I told him my property was in El Paso County. Which part of it is. This land straddles the original survey line, you see. The house and buildings are actually in El Paso, but the pasture and my garden are in Douglas."

Longarm coughed a little.

"I didn't mean any harm, you see. I simply thought the government doesn't need my money nearly so much as I do. So why pay property taxes to them? They only waste it anyway."

Longarm smiled. He didn't want to. He just couldn't help himself. If more taxpayers felt that way . . . well, it was just a damn good thing they didn't, that was all.

"They've left me alone since," Mrs. Parks concluded.

"And that's why you just went through the motions o' making out complaints when your steers disappeared, then turned t' Marshal Vail t' help you?" Longarm suggested.

"I knew Billy would think of some way he could help. And of course he did."

"Yes, ma'am."

"Can I assume you've solved my problem, Mr. Long?"

"Not exactly, ma'am. Not yet. Y'see, there's more to this than just somebody stealing a few cows. The way I see it, somebody likely wants t' force you off this ground. It's important to them. I've learned that much. This deal is bigger than the worth of a few skinny dairy steers. An' the only other thing I can think of is that it must be connected with the fact that your land ain't listed as bein' in either county. Prob'ly this person, whoever it is, has some swindle going an' needs t' be outside the jurisdiction o' either county sheriff's office. Now that sorta thing won't actually hold up. The courts wouldn't for a minute allow it. But your average criminals ain't half as bright as they think they are, an' they wouldn't know that. So more'n likely some assho . . . ah . . . imbecile has it in mind t' get hold o' your land an' set up some illegal scheme here. Thinking that if this land don't exist on government paper, then a fella could run here an' thumb his nose at pursuing deputies 'cause they wouldn't have jurisdiction an' couldn't follow across the line. They could be thinking this would be a no-man's-land, like. Free an' lawless. It wouldn't ever really work like that, of course. But I'd bet that's what somebody believes could happen. So I'm thinking the loss o' them steers was just intended t' pinch your pocketbook an' make it easier t' force you t' sell out to them. What I need from you, Miz Parks, is the name of whoever it is that's trying t' buy your place. Once I have that, you see, I'll have whoever it is that stole your steers an' has been trying t' put lead in my back."

Mrs. Parks gasped. "Someone has actually shot at you?"

"It's nothing for you t' worry about, ma'am. After all, they missed. But I'd rather they weren't left loose t' try again. So if you'd tell me who it is that's trying t' get your land away from you . . ."

Mrs. Parks gave him a blank look.

"Ma'am?" Longarm persisted.

"But . . . I'm sorry, Mr. Long. But no one has expressed interest in buying me out. Not once since Mr. Parks died. I can assure you, Mr. Long, if I ever got a fair offer for this property, I would sell it and be gone to live near my sister in Fort Worth before the ink on the deed had time to dry."

"Ma'am?" It was Longarm's turn to look blank.

"Really, Mr. Long. No one wants to buy this place. No one at all."

"But what about . . . ?" Shit. All that carefully devised line of logic. Shot to hell. But . . .

But if there was no one trying to acquire this officially nonexistent land parcel . . . then who . . . then why . . . damn!

Chapter 29

Longarm dismounted in front of Vance Hollowell's office and went inside. The El Paso County deputy was there, seated behind his desk with his often-injured leg propped on a padded stool. There was someone with him, a much younger man with freckles and ears as big as bat wings. The youngster wore a cheap, shapeless, sagging hat that looked like it was melting and boots that appeared to be older than he was. But the large-caliber revolver on his belt looked up-to-date and mighty well cared for.

"Longarm!"

"Don't try an' get up, Vance. No need t' jostle that leg o' yours."

"All right, but sit down. We were just talking about you."

"You were?"

"Sure were. Do you know Jason here?"

"Can't say that I've had the pleasure." Longarm smiled at the young man and extended his hand.

The youngster jumped to his feet and grinned. "This is a honor, sir. A real honor."

Longarm felt like visiting royalty or something. It wasn't exactly a common experience.

"Longarm, this here is my counterpart from across the county line, Jason Buddiger, Jason, Custis Long."

"My pleasure, Jason. Milt Selkirk speaks right highly o' you."

The boy looked like he might bust with pride. He grinned and blushed and likely would have wagged his tail if he'd known how. "I-I've heard l-lots about y-you, sir."

"Nobody went an' named me Sir, son. Whyn't you call me Longarm like the rest o' my friends do."

Longarm wouldn't have thought it possible, but Jason's grin became even wider.

"It's a convenient thing that you dropped in now, Longarm," Vance Hollowell said. "Jason came here looking for you. I was just giving him directions out to Mrs. Parks's place when you rode up."

"That so?"

"Yes, sir . . . I mean, yes, Longarm," Jason put in. "I got a wire from Milt this morning saying I should come see could I help you."

"You aren't needed in court right now?"

The boy—he was probably in his mid-twenties, but the combination of his freckles and an aw-shucks attitude made him seem much younger—chuckled. "The trial's ended. The Raines boys was convicted of kidnap and assault."

"And wait till you hear what else," Hollowell put in.

"Some smart so-an'-so on the jury turned a new wrinkle too," Jason said. "This guy must've sat through some trials before, I'd say. He knew about there being such a thing as a lesser included offense. So this jury up and convicted both Raines boys of horse theft too, since they took that coach horse for the lady to ride.

"The Raineses could get twenty-five years for the kidnap and another three to five for the assault, but danged if the jury didn't recommend hanging on the horse-theft charge they dreamed up themselves. Of course it was only because of what those boys done to the lady they kidnapped. Hadn't nothing to do with stealing horses. But it seems to be legal no matter how they come to do it."

"I never heard that one before," Longarm conceded. "Not without the prosecutor placing the charge."

"The judge hadn't neither, but you could see he liked the idea. Of course, even if he goes along with it and sentences them to hang it'll go up on appeal. It could be years before we know for sure what will happen. But it was kind of interesting. I'm glad I got to hear it."

"Sounds interesting," Longarm agreed.

"A lot more than most of what I get to do," Jason said. He grinned again. "You know, I always figured it was just us local fellas that had to put up with dull stuff. Now Vance has been telling me about you and Mrs. Parks." He laughed. "I reckon even important federal officers like you have to take on routine junk now and then."

"Huh," Longarm grunted. "Not as routine as I thought."

"No?"

He told them about the little matter of the missing jurisdiction—he'd already warned Mrs. Parks that he would, and had advised her to take care of it on her own before some picayune bureaucrat did it for her and maybe caused trouble for her while he was at it—and about the attempts on his life.

Jason frowned. "That doesn't sound right."

"How so?"

"Why, when the lady first told Milt about it and then he told me, I knew right off who had to be behind the loss of them steers."

"Oh?"

"Sure. Wasn't our case, of course, or at least we didn't think so at the time. But I sent a note to John Dumphries telling him if he needed help to let me know."

"Dumphries?" Longarm asked.

"He's the deputy who was in this office before I came in," Vance said. "I don't recall him mentioning anything about a note to me at the time. But then Johnny thought it wasn't our case to worry about. For that matter, he might not have gotten the note. When he left here he moved back to New Mexico someplace so he could be closer to his wife's folks. I don't know if his mail was forwarded or not. Jason's note wasn't in any of the files that were turned over to me, though. I'm sure of that."

"Bad timing," Longarm said, "but good intentions. Jason, you say you can help clear up this theft business if you're asked. Well, son, I'm asking."

Jason acted like an invitation to help Longarm was just about the nicest gift he'd received in a long time. "You bet, sir. I mean, Longarm. I can take you right to 'em."

"You want to go along, Vance?" Longarm asked.

"Not if you two don't need me. I don't feel much like forking a horse again for a while." He nodded in the direction of his wounded leg.

"Oh, we won't have to ride," Jason said. "I'm betting the boys we want are right here in Palmer Lake, not a quarter mile from where we're setting."

"In that case I'll amble along," Hollowell said. "If you'll go slow."

The three lawmen got up and left the El Paso County deputy's office. Slowly.

Chapter 30

Jason had been way off on his estimate of the distance involved. The place they wanted was less than two hundred yards away from Vance Hollowell's office. A sign over the front door read: "Piper Barnes and Son, Fine Meats." A smaller posting nearby added: "Custom Butchers, Processing Meats Domestic and Wild, Lowest Prices, Now in Our Second Generation of Satisfied Customers, Meating All Needs."

"Either of you boys know if that there is bad spelling or just bad humor?" Longarm asked. Neither of the others answered.

The three lawmen went inside. A plump woman with hair as white as her apron greeted them. "Vance, Jason, hello to you. And to you, mister. What can I get for you gentlemen today, please?"

"Is Curtis here, Mrs. Barnes?" Jason asked. He seemed to have taken charge for the time being. Longarm was certainly agreeable to that since Jason was the only one among them who seemed to know what was going on.

"Curt and his daddy are in the back."

"Thank you, ma'am." Jason smiled and touched the brim

of his floppy old hat. He motioned for Longarm and Vance to follow.

The back of the shop was divided into a large workroom with heavy tables, overhead hooks holding great chunks of meats and whole fowl, and another room at the back that, judging from the size and construction of its vaultlike door, was almost certainly a heavily insulated icehouse.

A middle-aged man and a younger fellow about Jason's age were busy at the work tables, the older man cutting beef while the younger one was cleaning chickens.

The workroom stank of blood and chickens. Longarm didn't much mind the blood, but he despised the stink of the chickens.

"Mr. Barnes," Jason said, nodding.

"Hello, Jason."

The younger Barnes, Curtis that would be, looked up with a scowl and offered no greeting.

"Curtis, this here is Deputy Marshal Long. He's a federal officer down from Denver. Did you know Mrs. Parks donated some of her steers to the United States government?"

"Now why would I know a thing like that?" Curtis sullenly grumbled.

"You should've known, Curtis, because that makes stealing her steers a federal crime. Did you know that?"

Curtis didn't say anything. His father began to puff up all red in the face.

"Are you accusing my son of something, Jason? Because if you are, young man, let me tell you something. You'll produce your proof or I'll run you right out of here. You have no business here anyway. Go on. Get out. Go back up to Douglas County where you belong. Deputy Hollowell, I demand that you order Jason out. This is private property, and he has no business here."

"I'm not so sure, Mr. Barnes. Jason and I are both cooperating with a federal officer in the pursuit of a criminal wanted by the federal government. I'm not real sure who can demand what, that being the case."

"I insist—"

"Tell you what, Mr. Barnes," Longarm put in. "This is your property, like you say. And it's your son been accused. Why don't you let us look around? If we don't find anything, why, that will prove to us that your son is innocent, and we'll go down the street an' all have us a drink together."

"Fuck you," the elder Barnes snapped.

Longarm smiled. "Y'know, Mr. Barnes, that kinda makes me think that if young Curt has done somethin', then his daddy was part an' parcel of it too."

"Get out. All of you. Right now."

"I don't know as we want t' do that just yet," Longarm said.

"Show me your search warrant," Barnes demanded. "You can't come in here without a search warrant, so get out." The man made the mistake of using a meat cleaver to gesture with.

Barnes waved the thing in the general direction of Longarm's face. And found himself doubled over on the ground with a fireball of raw pain where his nuts were dangling.

"Assaulting a federal officer, Mr. Barnes. A man could get two years for that. Maybe more."

Barnes groaned a little but didn't say much on the subject. Across the room his son was acting feisty too. But only a little.

"How many times have you and me snapped assholes at the Saturday night fandangos, Curtis?" Jason asked with a taunting grin.

Curtis didn't answer.

"Six? Eight maybe? How many of those did you win, Curtis?"

Again there was no response.

"Can you think of any? I can't. You want we should tangle again?"

Curtis shook his head.

"That's real smart of you, Curtis. Could it be that you're learning? Now if we can only get you to leave other people's livestock alone . . ." Jason turned to Longarm and said, "Curtis and his daddy sell meat real cheap. They can afford to because ol' Curtis here steals a lot of what they butcher. I thought I'd broke him of the habit a while back, but I guess I only got him to move his activities out of Douglas County. Sorry about that, Vance. I should've known better than to trust his promise. He swore he'd never steal nothing again if I let him go. My fault for believing him."

"You don't have anything on us," the senior Barnes said from his nest in the sawdust on the floor. "Nothing. And you don't have a search warrant either. So get out or I'll have my lawyer file a suit against each of you."

The SOB had them when it came to the lack of a warrant, Longarm conceded. And it would take until sometime tomorrow at the very earliest before he could find a federal judge and have a warrant duly sworn and submitted for service. By then any evidence now on these premises would be gone and buried deep.

Jason didn't look at all worried. He just grinned some more.

"Sorry, boys," Longarm said, "but this here is a federal matter, and our federal judges got no sense of humor. They like things done by the book or they'll disallow the charge. And the man is right. I got no warrant to search here."

"Me neither," Jason said, "but I'll bet I can think of a way Vance can search the place nice and legal. If El Paso County

156

does things like we do up in Douglas, anyway."

"How's that, Jason?" Hollowell asked.

"Does your sheriff do like ours and have every deputy given a commission as an assistant to the brand inspector?"

Hollowell brightened. And so did Longarm. Brand inspectors had the right to scrutinize any animal skin. And they did not need search warrants to do so. By the act of going into business as a butcher shop, Piper Barnes and Son had given the state an open invitation to inspect any hides on or about the property.

"Don't bother telling us where you keep your hides," Longarm said. "I don't reckon we'd much believe what you have t' say anyhow."

Not that direction was required anyway. The green hides were piled in a lean-to behind the butcher shop.

It remained to be seen how many of the hides could be accounted for by way of the bills of sale in Barnes's records.

What Longarm was looking for was easily found. The medium-brown hides of at least three jersey steers were in the pile, readily identifiable by their brand. The two freshest of those could logically be assumed to have belonged to the United States government.

"I'm placing both of you under arrest," Longarm told Barnes the father and Barnes the son.

"Damn," the older Barnes complained. "How much is this likely to cost us?"

"That's for a judge to decide, not me. It could mean jail time for you."

Barnes sneered. "No way, Marshal. I been in this business a long time. You aren't going to scare me that easy. A fine is what we'll get. And restitution. My lawyer will see to all that. Count on it. Curt, mind you don't give these bastards anything they can use against us in court. Mind you smile nice and do whatever they say." He raised his voice and called out, "Old woman, you get yourself over to Tom Fain's office. Tell him we're arrested and he's to come bail us out. Tell him I'm offering the same fee as before."

"You don't sound much worried," Longarm said.

"I'm not. You can't scare me, you know. I been around. You put me in jail this afternoon, I'll be back here cutting meat before my missus runs out of inventory. I won't miss a day of work nor a single sale because of this. Wait and see."

Longarm frowned. Not because he particularly gave a damn what happened to the Barneses and their business.

But because neither the father nor the son seemed to really mind all that much that they'd been caught.

Certainly neither of them acted like it meant enough to them that they would be willing to kill to protect their penny-ante little scheme here.

And if the Barneses hadn't been shooting at him over this cow-theft thing . . . then who the hell had? And why?

Chapter 31

Castle Rock. That was where he'd first encountered this unknown gunman with the shotgun. It was the town the shooter seemed familiar with. Longarm was going back to Castle Rock.

Technically speaking his case was successfully ended, and he probably ought to go back to Denver and report in.

But dammit, he just didn't much like the thought of letting someone take two whacks at him and get away with it.

And Castle Rock was right on the way to Denver. Surely Billy wouldn't object if Longarm had himself a little layover on his way home.

He turned the prisoners over to Jason Buddiger along with a note to Marshal Vail—Jason seemed pleased as punch to be asked a favor by the respected deputy from Denver—and rode back to the Lark Ranch so he could return the mare to Cathy Sue.

He was halfway hoping the gunman would make another try for him, but ever since he'd left the train at Monument the feeling of being watched had been absent. It didn't come back on the ride to the Lark place either.

"I appreciate all your help, John," Longarm told his old friend. "And yours, Cathy Sue."

"You'll stay the night with us, of course," John Lark offered.

"Thanks, John, but I gotta be on my way. Gotta get back, y'know." The truth was that he didn't want to stay there and risk endangering John and Cathy Sue if the gunman should show up.

And there was an addendum to that truth as well, it being that if he spent the night there again he was certain to find Cathy Sue in his bed once more. That would've been plenty nice enough of itself—after all, he liked the girl mighty well—except that it would only go and make him feel guilty all over again about making himself free with a friend's daughter. That was a pendulum-swing of emotions that he could right happily do without, he decided.

"What I would appreciate," Longarm said, "is a ride back down t' the railroad. If you got anybody goin' that way, that is." He wouldn't have asked if he hadn't already noticed the hired hand hitching a team to the light wagon. That generally meant a trip to town was in the works, and Longarm didn't really care which town was being visited. If it was a shopping trip up to Castle Rock, that would put him right where he wanted to be. And if there was ranch business to be done in Palmer Lake that would be fine too; he could take a coach over to Monument and connect with the train there.

"I could drive him, Daddy," Cathy Sue volunteered so quickly that Longarm was afraid her father would suspect the truth.

"No, honey, Benny is going anyway. Custis can ride with him."

Cathy Sue pouted but, fortunately, stopped short of making a real fuss. She did give Longarm a yearning look behind her father's back, but he pretended not to see that.

And contrived as well to not be alone with her until he was safely perched on the passenger's seat in the spring wagon with a taciturn Benny handling the reins.

"You come back, Custis. Promise me."

"I will, Cathy Sue. I promise." He neglected to specify exactly when that would be.

"Anytime," her father added. "You know you're welcome."

Longarm smiled and tugged at the brim of his Stetson. When Benny pulled out of the yard Longarm wasn't sure if he was more relieved . . . or more horny.

Whichever, he quickly put Cathy Sue and John Lark out of mind.

There were other things he needed to be thinking about right now.

Chapter 32

The feeling was back. In spades. For two days and part of a third he'd been farting around in Castle Rock, showing himself in the courthouse, in the saloons, in hotel lobbies, in any public place he could think of where he could make himself visible.

What he was doing, although he hoped no one else knew it, was offering himself for bait.

And now, by damn, it looked to be paying off.

The predator was moving in on the bait, sniffing the air and sneaking closer.

Longarm could feel it in the prickly sensations at the back of his neck and in the tightness that pulled at his temples. He held himself straighter and taller, and there was a sense of swollen fullness across his shoulders and through his chest. His cods hung high and tight, and he was ready to fight anything or anyone that crossed him.

He flexed the fingers of his gun hand and stepped off the sidewalk into the mouth of an alley.

It was daylight, the middle of the afternoon, but that didn't mean the gunman wasn't interested. The sonuvabitch was close. Longarm *knew* he was.

The question was whether the shooter would try now or later.

But he would try. Longarm knew he would. Wanted him to. Was damn well depending on him to try one more time.

Damn him to hell anyway.

Longarm crossed the mouth of the trash-strewn alley, the tension so tight in him that he was about to explode into action with or without the presence of an actual threat.

But he contained himself, somehow, and went on down the damn street without anything happening.

Yet.

After dark then, he told himself. The gunman couldn't wait much longer.

And neither could Longarm.

He had supper at a place where the food was lousy but where there were few other customers to be endangered. Ever since he'd returned to Castle Rock he'd avoided seeing Celeste for fear she might be caught in the line of fire if . . . when . . . something happened. He'd avoided Milt Selkirk and Jason Buddiger too for fear that their presence might scare the gunman away.

Longarm wanted this guy. For reasons both professional and personal.

He ate alone and then, once dusk gave way to the silences of the night, went out onto the street again.

Not into the saloons this time. Too crowded.

The back of his neck tingled, and a muscle at the corner of his left eye twitched.

He walked down the sidewalk, his boots sounding hollow and very loud as they struck the boards, in the direction of the railroad depot and loading pens.

Castle Rock was proud of being a modern town. Gaslights illuminated the business district. Longarm passed under the last of the lights and walked on into the shadows.

A herd of cattle had been delivered to the rail-side pens sometime during the day. Longarm could hear the clatter of horn on horn as the beeves crowded together. He could smell fresh urine and sun-baked manure and the warm, pleasant scent of living cow flesh.

And he could feel the presence of the man who wanted to kill him.

Close. The shooter was very close.

Longarm reached the corral rails and followed along them in the direction of the roadbed and the massive, sturdy loading chutes.

Moonlight was the only illumination here. A cloud drifted across the face of the pale and distant moon, blocking off what little light there was. Longarm ducked under the ramp of the first chute and came up on the other side, startling a cow that was separated from him by the width of a thick oak plank. The cow bawled and darted sideways, bumping into another cow with a hiss of forcibly expelled breath. There was a thump of hoofs and the clicking of horns as the cattle inside the pen tried to jump away from each other in the too-close confinement of the corral.

The cloud slid off the face of the moon like a theater light with the shutter being drawn back.

There!

The figure was distinct in the darkness. Black on charcoal. But distinct. Upright. Drooping hat brim. Stubby, black-as-Lucifer's-soul object held canted across the chest and belly . . . the shotgun seen in uncertain silhouette.

But Longarm knew. He knew.

And so did the man with the gun.

The shotgun came up. Pointing. Lethal. The range closer than Longarm would have believed it possible for anyone to get without being seen before now.

The shotgun came up.

But it was Longarm's Colt that spoke first.

A sheet of fire lighted up the rough timber of the loading

164

chute and sent the beeves into a frenzy of sudden panic. Their hoofs sounded like thunder, and the corral rails groaned and creaked as the cattle tried to escape.

Longarm's night vision was destroyed. He stared ahead, blinded, even while he dropped into a crouch behind the protection of the loading chute.

He heard a cry of pain.

Real? It could as easily be feigned. He blinked and with his free hand rubbed at his eyes, knowing that would do nothing to speed the restoration of his night vision, but doing it anyway out of a sense of urgency.

The shotgun hadn't been fired. The gunman had been looking into the muzzle flash of Longarm's .44, though. Surely his vision was ruined too.

But which of them would recover quicker?

Longarm kept low and felt his way along the side of the loading chute to its end beside the gleaming steel of the railroad tracks.

Gleaming. He could see the pale silver of moonlight reflecting on the steel. Not well, but he could see. Good. He held his Colt ready and tried to reach out with his ears to find the shooter and figure out what he was up to.

He could hear sobbing. Faked? Possibly. He blinked again and looked around. His vision was nearly back to normal now. He peered around the end of the loading chute.

There. On the ground. Was that a body? Or merely a shadow? He couldn't be sure.

It moved. He could see the movement and heard the subdued sound of something heavy shifting on gravel at the same time.

Was that the shooter then? Down? He thought so.

He was not going to bet his life on it.

He waited, silent and still and patient, where he was, Colt poised in his hand.

"Help me. God a'mighty, you gotta help me." The shooter sounded bad. To Longarm's thinking, that was good.

"Mister. You gotta help me. You gut-shot me."

Longarm said nothing. He could see fairly well again now. He glanced up to make sure there were no other clouds moving into a position that would obscure the light again in the next few minutes.

"Deputy? Deputy Long? I know it's you. You got to help me. You got to get me to a doctor. I'm dying. You got to help me."

"Throw the gun toward the tracks," Longarm said, breaking his silence for the first time.

"I can't move. I can't do that."

"Fine by me, fucker. Lay there an' die then."

Longarm saw the shotgun tumbled end over end to land with a clatter on the rock ballast of the railroad tracks.

"Now your pistol."

"I got no pistol."

"Bullshit."

A pistol spun through the air and landed noisily on the rocks.

"Now crawl to your right about four yards. You're in the shadows there. I want t' see you."

"I can't move."

"Your choice."

"You son of a bitch," the shooter whined.

"Like I say . . . your choice."

A moment later the wounded gunman crawled into the moonlight, moving forward a bit at a time like an oversized inchworm crawling across the ground.

"That's fine. Hold your hands over your head where I can see them. Both of them, dammit. If you hold onto your belly like that I can't tell if you have a hideout gun or not."

"You bastard."

166

"Do it."

Longarm straightened, the tension ebbing quickly now, and took long strides forward to kneel by the wounded man's side and check him quickly for weapons. Longarm's touch encountered the warm wetness of blood but no threat of cold steel.

He pulled out a cheroot and clamped it between his teeth. He struck a match, and before he lighted the smoke held the flame low so he could get a decent look at the shooter. Longarm frowned. He'd seen this prick before. On the depot platform down in Colorado Springs. Except then the guy had been a "sleeping" cowboy lounging on a bench. Shit. He'd been good at his deception. Good enough that Longarm had bought the play. Damn him.

Longarm moved the flame lower so he could see the wound, then brought it up to light his cheroot. The smoke tasted clean in his throat. He enjoyed the flavor of it for a moment, then slowly exhaled.

"All right," he said softly, "you and me have got to have us a talk."

"A doctor. I need a doctor."

"Yes, you do," Longarm agreed. "A doc can save you." Longarm's bullet hadn't missed the gunman's navel by more than half an inch. Longarm's guess was that there wasn't a doctor—hell, there wasn't a whole medical college of doctors— that could save this SOB from a screaming-painful end. But this didn't seem like a real good time to speculate about that out loud. "Soon as you tell me what I want to know I'll go fetch a doctor for you." That was no lie. Longarm had no interest in causing more pain for the shooter. It was enough to have killed him. And if a doctor could give the gunman something to mute the pain, that would be all right.

"I need . . ."

"Quick as you tell me what I want to know. That's a promise."

167

The shooter began to cry while he lay on the ground holding himself with both hands as if to keep his belly from splitting open and spilling his intestines out. He rocked back and forth a little.

And then, between sobs, he began to talk.

Chapter 33

Longarm dismounted and walked to the edge of the dropoff. A rock face that was as sheer and slick as the side wall of a barn cut away beneath the toes of his boots. The view from the top of the mesa was exhilarating, stretching far and pretty all the way to the mountains to the west.

Most of the rolling land he could see was a shadow-speckled yellow-brown as the grasses dried and stem-cured.

Over to the southwest, though, he could see a pocket of startling emerald.

That would be the spring the houseman had told him about. Pretty much had to be.

Longarm stayed on the mesa top no longer than necessary for him to take a few bearings that would guide him to the hidden spring, then returned to the horse he'd rented in Castle Rock and took it down the easy east slope as fast as the stony ground surface allowed.

He turned west again then and began lining up the bearings. The spring, concealed in a depression at the northwest corner of a small mesa and surrounded by lush grass and drooping cottonwoods, was no trouble to reach after that.

The senator and his lady were there where he'd been told

to expect them. They had a quilt laid out, and picnic baskets waited close by.

Longarm thought both the senator and his fiancée looked a mite red in the face and breathless when he joined them, but they were both fully dressed. After all, they'd had plenty of time to hear him approach. As he'd fully intended. He didn't want to piss off Senator Walker any more than he absolutely had to.

"Senator. Ma'am." He touched the brim of his hat.

"Longarm. I certainly didn't expect to see you here."

"No, sir, I reckon you wouldn't."

"I am sure you have a good reason, though. Assuming this encounter is no accident."

"No, sir, it's not an accident. Mind if I step down?"

"Please do. We, um, were just about to see what the cook sent us for lunch. I'm sure there will be enough for three."

"Thank you, sir, but I've already eaten." He hadn't, but accepting a meal from the gentleman didn't seem the right thing to do just now. He swung down from his saddle and tied the horse to the back of the senator's buggy.

"Would you care for a glass of champagne, Marshal?" Miss Gayle offered in a too-sweet voice. Longarm knew good and well she hadn't forgiven him for rejecting her before; she was being nice for the senator's benefit, not Longarm's. Under the circumstances that was just fine by him.

"No, thank you, Lily."

The senator gave Longarm a sharp look. "I say now. I don't recall anyone inviting you to make yourself so free with the lady's name, Long."

"No, sir, but there seems t' be a mite o' confusion on that point."

"What point is that, Long?"

"The, um, lady's name, sir."

"Come again?"

"Your fiancée, sir. Her name ain't Lillith Gayle. Or at least it wasn't for the past couple years. She ever mention she used t' live in Omaha?"

The senator looked confused. "Dear?"

Lily looked like she was apt to bite nails in two. Or tear Longarm's heart out of his chest.

"Her name back in Omaha, Senator, was Gail Gilden, sometimes known as Lily or the Gilded Lily or just plain Lil."

"But . . ."

"You bastard," Lily hissed.

"Funny thing, Lily. Your brother called me that too. Just last night."

"You saw . . . where is he? What have you done with him, damn you?"

"I don't understand what's going on here," the senator complained. Neither Longarm nor Miss Gilden was paying much attention to him at that moment, however.

"Is he . . . ?"

"Dead? Nope. Not the last I saw him anyhow." That was true enough. The man had been dying at the time but not yet dead. Longarm had no way to tell what the SOB's condition would be by now, of course.

"You're either lying to me about that or you're trying to run a bluff on me."

"Neither one, lady. Your brother peached. Opened right up, he did."

"Please," Senator Walker said. "Will one of you tell me what is going on here?"

"Pretty simple, Senator. Your pretty fiancée, who isn't at all who or what you thought, figured t' use you t' step up in the world. Figured marrying you would make her respectable. A helluva long climb that woulda been, but she thought she could pull it off."

"Don't," Lily said. "Please."

171

Longarm ignored her. "Back in Omaha, Senator, she was a whore. Not even a fancy whore, she was just a fifty-cent barroom screw. I bet back then she didn't know how t' dress and make herself up pretty, though. I bet if she had, why, she'd've been worth a dollar, maybe two bucks a throw."

The woman launched herself at Longarm. He slapped her hands down and captured her wrists, spinning her around so she couldn't knee him in the balls, which she was most earnestly trying to accomplish.

"She's a wild one, Senator. Hell, it woulda been all right too. Nobody woulda cared really. Except she was so fretful that you might discover who she was that she made a big mistake. A young fella name of David Pembrooke used to know Lily in Omaha. Then—an' this part I'm guessing about—somehow he ran into her again here. Her or her brother, it don't much matter which. Point is, Pembrooke knew who Lily used t' be. So when he got himself thrown in jail, he sent her word that she'd best find a way to get him out or else he'd spill the beans about her past. I see that name means something to you, Senator."

"Of course, it's . . . I mean . . ."

"It's the young fella she talked you into trying to get moved from federal court to state. We thought it had something t' do with politics. Instead it had t' do with love. Or some version of it, anyway. She wanted you t' get Pembrooke tried in a local court so you could influence the judge or whoever an' get him off. The funny thing was that my boss Billy Vail was only reluctant t' let the case go because he didn't think the boy deserved risking the heavier penalties a state court could impose. He was tryin' t' be nice to the blackmailer. Ain't that a hoot, Senator?"

"But I didn't . . . I mean, Lillith never . . ."

"You didn't know, Senator. I realize that. Nobody will blame you."

"Really though, Long, no harm has been done. Now that I

172

do know, we'll just forget this whole business with Pembrooke. He poses no threat to Lillith now. He can't harm her by telling me what I already know. And Lillith, why didn't you trust me to start with? Why ever would you be afraid of anything that young man could say? Don't you know by now that I love you? I would do anything for you. Anything. Truly. I . . . I care about your past. Of course I do. But it isn't anything that I can't forgive. I love you. None of that matters now. Let the federal courts prosecute Pembrooke. And let him say anything he wants. We won't let any of that bother us, dearest. Once you are Mrs. Walker, no one would dare insinuate anything about you. No one."

The woman stopped struggling against Longarm's grip and gave Walker a look of blank stupefaction. "You really . . ."

"Of course, darling. How could you not know that? How could you ever doubt our love?"

"You really are a dumb shit, George," the lovely young lady groaned.

Walker looked like he'd been slapped in the face. In a manner of speaking, of course, he had.

"What she ain't mentioning, Senator, is that she and her brother carried their game a mite too far t' ignore at this point."

"I don't understand," the senator said.

"No, sir, I don't expect you could. Y'see, it wasn't so bad when they tried t' use your influence t' get Pembrooke off. But when I showed up at your house to serve a subpoena to one of your hands—which I admit might of seemed like an excuse—she and her brother panicked. They thought I was really there investigating *them*. It was their own guilt that was spooking them, of course. But they thought I was onto them. An' the only way that could be, they figured, was if Pembrooke had already opened up. Partway, anyhow. I'm thinking there's more to this story than just the fact that Lily used t' take in

173

boarders between her legs. Like something plenty illegal Lily an' the brother were mixed up in too. Anyway, for whatever reason, they got real scared. They paid some fella in the Denver jail t' kill Pembrooke before he could say any more. An' then the idiot brother tried t' knock me off too. Twice. So now, Senator, there's charges o' murder, attempted murder, hell, maybe some other stuff too, all hanging over her an' the brother both. At the very least, Senator, Miss Lily here will be goin' behind bars for an awful long time. Could be she'll swing, though I doubt that. Life in prison is more likely."

"No," Walker said, trembling.

"Sorry, sir, but some things you just can't gloss over. I reckon murder is real high on that list."

"No," the senator repeated.

"I'll see she's not treated any worse than she has t' be, Senator. I can promise you that much." Longarm turned to guide Lily Gilden, or Lillith Gayle if she preferred—he certainly didn't give a crap which name she used—to the buggy. He figured he would have to borrow the buggy to get his prisoner back to Castle Rock. It wouldn't much do to make her walk.

He went to help her into the buggy.

Then he heard a flurry of sudden motion close behind him.

Chapter 34

Longarm heard the impact more than he felt it. It sounded hollow—but very close and personal—as something hard and heavy crashed into the back of his skull. A rock, a fist, what it was didn't matter.

He heard it hit, and the entire world took on a fuzzy, detached sort of indifference to him.

His knees buckled, and he hit the ground very hard. He knew he was falling, knew it when he hit the earth, knew that bits of sharp gravel were digging into his cheek. That seemed of passing interest but no real importance.

He could still feel. Sort of. And hear. He just no longer really cared.

"George. Dearest." For some reason that seemed faintly amusing, although at the moment he couldn't decide why it should.

"Hurry, Lillith."

"He isn't dead, George."

"Of course he isn't, darling."

"Well?"

"What?"

"Finish him, of course."

"Lillith!"

"Damn it, George, if you won't do it, I will. Give me your gun."

"No, darling. That would be murder."

"If he lives, George, I'm the one who will be wanted for murder."

"And if he doesn't, we both will. That wouldn't accomplish anything."

"He knows . . ."

"Lillith! Get into the buggy. I insist."

"But it would only take a minute to . . ."

"Now, Lillith. I insist. I love you. God help me, I do. But I'll not commit murder and I'll not allow you to. Now get into the buggy. We have to get away."

"But . . ."

"We have to hurry. We'll . . . we'll go somewhere. Start over under new names. I have money. I can get that from the bank. All my accounts. We'll have everything in the Castle Rock bank and in some accounts in Denver that you don't know about."

"Really, George?"

"But we have to hurry, Lillith. We have to get away before Long comes to."

"It would be easier if we just killed him, Georgie-bear."

"No more talk like that. Besides, look at him. He's out. Maybe he won't wake up again. Maybe he's dead already or dying. But we can't take any chances. We have to hurry. Go on now. Get in there. I'll get the hitch weights. Hurry."

There was a crunching of feet on gravel and the squeaking protest of springs, then the crack of a whip and the sound of iron tires grinding into the ground as the buggy moved away.

Longarm had the vague impression that he should get up now.

But it would be nice to go to sleep too.

Yes, the thought of sleep was very enticing indeed.

He closed his eyes and wished the damn flies would quit trying to feed on the blood that was matting his hair at the back of his head. The flies were bothersome, damn them. They wouldn't let him sleep.

Chapter 35

Jesus, his head hurt. He pulled the horse to a stop—funny thing how Walker'd untied the horse and left it behind; canny sonuvabitch of a politician always thinking ahead; if Longarm survived no one could charge Walker either with murder or with horse theft; if there was a live witness there couldn't be a capital sentence; canny sonuvabitch—and leaned over to puke. The heaving made his head pound, but he felt somewhat better afterward.

He looked up toward the sun and tried to gauge how much of a head start Walker and the girl had on him.

Too much for him to make it to Castle Rock before they had time to close the senator's bank accounts there and board the next train for Denver.

If only there was some way . . .

Whoa, now. Maybe there was.

Longarm turned the horse and—wincing—bumped it into a slow lope and then, when it'd had time to warm up, on into a run.

Not north to Castle Rock but due west.

He felt a trifle dizzy when he dismounted, but it was nothing he couldn't handle. The pounding in his head was much worse than the dizziness. But even that was less than it had been.

He stared down at the switch box. The damn thing was locked. Why hadn't that conductor Ned told him it would be locked?

For a few moments Longarm stood there peering stupidly down at the offending padlock. Then, forcibly rousing himself, he dragged out his revolver and shattered the lock with two carefully aimed shots.

Force of habit prompted him to replace the spent cartridges in his cylinder before he bent over—a mistake; he knelt instead and found that posture much more comfortable—and opened the steel door that was now somewhat battered.

There. The red boxes. He pulled one out and blinked at the words that danced and swam on the surface. Mm, right. Booms, Ned had called them. Signal bombs. Put 'em on the tracks, Ned had said. Longarm remembered that much.

But out in which direction? He didn't know which way the next train would be moving.

Didn't matter, he finally worked out through the cobwebs that were making a pudding of his brain. Take the horse. Lay booms on the rails in both directions. How far out? He couldn't recall. A ways. Fuck it. Put a bunch o' the damn things on the rails in both directions. Damn engineer would surely figure all those fireworks meant he oughta stop the train.

Longarm tucked a full box of signal bombs into each side pocket of his coat and laboriously scaled the cliff face that was the side of the damned horse. Tallest horse he'd ever seen. *Big* sum'bish. Don't fall now. Giddiyup, horse.

"Are you sure you're all right now, Longarm?"

"Lots better now, thanks."

"More coffee?"

"Yes to the coffee, no to the flask. I haven't gotten so many

179

wits back together that I can afford t' squander any at this here point."

"I will say you look a damn sight better'n you did when we found you."

"I feel better too, thanks t' you." Longarm reached for his watch and observed the time, then concluded that the calculations involved in working out the difference between now and the conductor's estimated time of arrival were beyond him. "How long now, Jerry?"

The conductor checked his own timepiece. "Eleven minutes."

Longarm grunted his thanks and rubbed his belly, surreptitiously checking to make sure the butt of the Colt was placed exactly where he liked it.

Not that he expected trouble. But still . . . He closed his eyes.

"I can see the mile marker ahead, Longarm. Castle Rock coming up."

Longarm stood. "Thanks, Jerry."

Chapter 36

Longarm stood in the doorway of the passenger coach. The conductor had assured him that the engineer would position the coach so that it was closest to the depot, and that the porters in the other cars would keep those doors shut. Passengers trying to embark at Castle Rock would necessarily have to board this coach.

As an additional precaution, even though George Walker already had demonstrated he was not the murderous type, all the northbound passengers who had been in this coach were now crowded into the other three passenger cars farther back.

No one would be permitted to leave the train at Castle Rock. Not right away, that is.

There had been mild grumbling but no real hostility aboard the train once Longarm displayed his badge. If anything, most of the D&RG passengers seemed to regard the event as a form of exciting entertainment. Longarm was sure, even though he'd asked them not to, that the windows of the coaches toward the rear of the train were crowded now with gaping onlookers.

The train slowed with a hiss of steam and a squeal of brakes but with little noise or jolting. The engineer was a remarkably able fellow, Longarm thought.

The coach door was placed within a few feet of where Longarm had asked for it to be. And this while the engineer in his cab was a good fifty, sixty yards farther north. The man really was good.

The coach porter sang out, "Castle Rock. All out for Castle Ro-ock!" and dropped lightly down to set the steel steps in place. Uncharacteristically, though, instead of remaining there to assist passengers up the steps, the porter trotted off in the direction of the stationmaster's office.

A young woman with two small boys clinging to her skirts climbed into the car. And found herself being whisked out of that coach and into another.

Two businessmen in deep conversation came aboard. And were immediately hustled away in confusion.

A distinguished gentleman with a pert and pretty young woman on his arm reached the foot of the steps.

And found Custis Long glaring down at him.

"The fun's over, Senator. You and the lady are both under arrest."

George Walker blanched. "How could you . . . ?"

"I'll tell you all about it, but not right now. Turn around, please. Hands behind your back." Longarm jumped down to the platform—he was pleased to discover that the jar of landing caused only a mild stab of pain in the back of his head—and reached for his handcuffs.

Senator Walker submitted himself to the manacles without complaint. He seemed resigned to capture now that he was facing a hale and healthy Longarm. All the fight had drained out of him.

"Now you, ma'am." Longarm had no more cuffs, but he would find something to immobilize her until he could borrow another pair from someone here in town.

"Of course, Marshal. I . . . oh, dear." Something fell from her hand and fluttered toward the platform.

Only a handkerchief. Nothing more threatening than that. Although naturally Longarm's attention was fixed on the falling object until he could identify it.

When he looked up again he was looking into the barrel of a palm gun with a flat, rotating cylinder instead of a revolving one. He had no idea where she could have been hiding the damned squeeze-gun.

"Still trying," he observed.

"Succeeding too, thank you," she said.

"Lillith . . ."

"Shut up, George. And don't stand so close. If I have to shoot him I don't want you getting in my way."

"Lillith . . ."

"Stop bleating, George. You sound like a sheep."

"But, dear . . ."

Sweet Lily was no longer paying attention to her erstwhile fiancé and lover. "Drop the gunbelt, Marshal. And need I remind you that unlike Georgie-bear I won't hesitate to kill you?"

"No reminder necessary," Longarm said. Meekly he unbuckled his belt and set it onto the railcar steps behind him.

"That's better. Now . . ."

"We should talk about this, Lily. We can work something out. Mind if I smoke?"

"Watch it!"

"No tricks. See?" Smiling, he pulled the lapel of his coat back so she could see there was no gun hidden there. Gingerly he plucked a cheroot out of his inside coat pocket and bit the end off it.

"No tricks," he repeated as he dipped two fingers into his vest pocket.

Lily's eyes went wide and her face pale as Longarm pulled out not a match but a brass-framed derringer brazed to the end of his watch chain.

Startled, she tried to shoot.

But her luck was no better than her brother's had been.

Longarm's derringer barked loudly. And its bite was vicious.

A pellet of heated lead smashed into her flesh in the delicate hollow that lay between her larynx and breastbone.

A gout of bright blood shot out of her slender body, arcing high and splashing onto the waistcoat of the senator from Douglas County.

Her gun clattered unfired to the platform decking, and a moment later she toppled down atop it.

"My God," George Walker wailed. "You've murdered a lady."

Longarm tucked the derringer away and picked up his gunbelt. Before buckling it in place he paused to pull out a match and light the cheroot that was still clamped in his jaw. "Wrong," he said as he puffed on the smoke. "Wrong on both counts. 'Twasn't murder. And she wasn't no damn lady."

On the platform around them the curious began to step out of hiding and crowd close to ooh and ahh over the sight of the dead woman.

Beside Longarm, George Walker began to shudder and weep.

Watch for

LONGARM AND THE TAOS TERROR

170th novel in the bold Longarm series
from Jove

Coming in February!

LONGARM

Explore the exciting Old West with
one of the men who made it wild!